HITO

Hito

An addictive gaming mystery

CAMERON LAWRENCE

Thurl Press

Acknowledgements

Anna Bowles
Edward Mortimer
Rose Lawrence
Lauren Tudor

Contents

Contents ~ ix

Chapter 1

The Game

Ryan clicked the yellow flashing MSN icon at the bottom of the screen. This is life in 2005. You spend all day at school and then come home and chat to the same friends on MSN; or in Ryan's case, just one friend.

Cali: *Sorry about what happened today.*

He read the message and grimaced as he replayed the event in his head. As he strode to art class, the only lesson he enjoyed, he didn't see the sandwich that was flying through the air towards him. It hit him squarely on the head. He recoiled and let out a confused grunt, before looking down to see it on the floor in two halves. Roars of laughter erupted across the yard. His face maroon as he hastily escaped to the cover of the classroom.

He shuffled in his computer chair, reliving the full embarrassment.

Cali: *Take your mind off it. Play some Hito*

Ryan: *Hito???*

Cali: *Idiot. It's the game I've told you about. Even Gabby was on about it in English Lit.*

Gabby played Hito? It was hard to imagine that the most popular girl at school would be interested in playing a video game. It wasn't going to hurt him to play it; in fact, he might be good at it. Maybe it would help him become popular at school.

His glasses caught the glare from the desktop PC that stood in the corner of his attic room. Cali sent through a link, and he clicked. Ominous sci-fi music blared from his computer. He lurched from his seat to turn the speakers off before his parents came up from downstairs. He stared at the screen. Dark blue flooded it like the tide. The word *Hito* etched in a Japanese-style font appeared in one of the waves. Ryan clicked the word and then a pop-up asked him to type in his name.

"Sorry, Ryan is already taken. Please enter a different name."

He settled for Ryan2005 and moved through to the "Create Your Hito" page. Ryan re-created his look as accurately as he could. Pale face, bulky glasses, average height and build, freckles and a chin that protruded not nearly as much as what it should. He even managed to add an anonymous polo-shirt to his hito. A polo-shirt that looked like one of the many that hung in his wardrobe.

Cali: *You still not ready?*

Ryan: *Sorry, I was just finishing my "hito" lol. Going through now.*

Ryan's hito landed in a room that was almost church-like. About a hundred people – hitos – were standing around randomly, some seemingly on top of each other, with speech bubbles appearing above each head as they typed a message to the group. He looked around for Cali's hito. With his copper curly hair, he shouldn't be too hard to find. He scrolled over a hito on the far left of the screen and saw him. His hair ablaze. His build similar to Ryan's, but his dress sense far more adventurous for someone geeky. A patchwork denim jacket paired with skinny black jeans. As Cali's mum always warned him, he looked like he could be in one of those rock bands that are destined for hell. Though Cali questioned whether his Ghanaian mother had ever listened to a rock band in her life.

"Hello," "Hi," "Hey everyone" appeared in the speech bubbles above heads, with no real conversation. In the real world, Ryan scratched his smooth chin, confused as to why people enjoyed this game. Why not just chat on MSN? A pigeon was sitting on the ledge of his attic window. Cooing as it scuffled around looking for any food in between the cracks of the tiles. The room lit up and his eyes flicked back to the screen to see that another pop-up had opened.

"Are you ready to enter Hito?"

Ryan lazily, unenthusiastically clicked *yes*. He could either play this lame game or watch the pigeon outside. The screen faded to black, and a loading bar filled the screen. Green crawled along the progress bar. 10% to Hito. 20% to Hito. Clicking the mouse didn't help with speeding things up. The bar finally reached 100% and Ryan wormed eagerly in his seat.

"Please switch on your speakers," the screen read. Ryan did so reluctantly, and a female voice began speaking in a soft, friendly American accent. An accent you would never hear in Thurlcaster, filled only with the richest of Northern accents.

"Welcome to Hito...

You'll shortly be paired up with another hito...

You'll earn points, or buki as we call them here, for every action and interaction within the Hito universe...

It's up to you to figure out what results in the most buki...

You can only play one connection session per day...

Good luck, fellow hito."

Ryan leaned closer to the screen as the image changed and he saw the hito he created standing in a grassy field. The emerald green stretched for miles, with shallow rolling hills and wooden fencing creating a picturesque British countryside setting. Clouds symmetrically lined the sky. He dragged up the MSN window.

Ryan: *Where are you? I'm in some kind of field.*

Cali: *Lol I think I've had that scene. I'm in a factory. Anyone with you yet?*

Ryan: *Nope. Just me.*

He rolled the mouse and the view swivelled around to his left. He panned the perspective to look behind him and there stood a girl with messy blond hair. She was wearing a polka dot dress that looked just right in this rural location. He hovered over her hito but only faded out grey boxes appeared.

"Hello, I'm Ryan," he typed hesitantly and pressed enter, not knowing if the stranger would reply.

"Hi, asl?" she responded swiftly.

"14, male, Thurlcaster, UK. You?"

"I'm Amy. 15. Female. Leicester. Let's explore?"

Was she telling the truth about her age and location? He didn't know; it was very easy to lie online. But either way he was keen to explore this new universe. The pigeon sat on the roof ledge, still searching for its dinner, occasionally pecking the windowpane. Ryan didn't notice.

After fidgeting with the mouse and keyboard, Ryan followed Amy through the grassy field, the long stems grazing her bare legs. A river meandered along beside them as the summer sun blazed down. They arrived at what he first thought was a cottage, but as he got closer, realised it was a watermill sitting on the river. The wooden structure spun smoothly, scooping water up with every degree it turned. The sound of the water sounded so realistic that it could have tricked him had he been looking away from the screen.

"Follow me," Amy said.

She lunged onto the water wheel and rode it until she reached the top, then slid effortlessly through the top window of the mill. Ryan pressed the right, left and middle buttons on the mouse, before trying the arrow buttons on his keyboard. He finally managed to step onto the wheel, and then used the down arrow to awkwardly crouch and jump in through the window, though he nearly missed it and fell into the river. He stood facing her hito. The bare room had pine panels for walls, ceilings and floors.

"Have you played this game much?" Amy said.

The pride in Ryan didn't want to admit that he was new to this world. "No, I've played it quite a bit."

"Show me your face," Amy said.

He wheeled his chair a little closer to the screen and re-read the message. He started typing and three dots appeared above his hito, and then deleted it before sending. Then he did it again.

"You can see my face. What do you mean show my face?" Ryan typed back after much internal deliberation, confused as to why she was asking.

"No, your real face."

Ryan's spine tingled. The bare room felt like a prison cell, and he was going to have to reply to this strange girl. What was this game? How could you possibly earn points from standing around in a mill with a weirdo?

"I don't think I can show you on here. And why would I!?"

The pigeon had now already flown away from the window, but Ryan hadn't noticed as he was too engrossed in the game. Nor did he realise that the red light on the webcam clipped to the top of his screen had now turned on.

"Oh, you actually do look like your hito," Amy said, "The same glasses and the same polo-shirt. Strange."

Ryan looked up to see the red light on the camera. He yanked the webcam, ripping its cable out of the back of the computer. His heart pounding, throwing it into the middle of the floor. He collapsed back into the chair. On screen, his hito was still standing in the mill. His blood raced as he typed a message to Amy, squinting back at the screen through his glasses. She was gone.

The wood-panelled room faded to black. He pressed a few buttons to see if he could go back. It didn't work.

The ominous music played again as text appeared on the screen.

100 buki earned. Position: 1,762,041.

Ryan scrolled down and clicked the MSN tab at the bottom of his screen. Cali's status was already offline, so he shut down the PC and then uncomfortably lay in bed. He wondered what Amy's agenda was, and how she managed to switch on his webcam. Moonlight shone through the window, and he reluctantly glanced at the webcam in the middle of the floor.

Even though it was unplugged from the computer, he feared he was still being spied on. Expecting the red light to be watching him whilst he slept.

Chapter 2

Gabby

Everyone hated English Literature lessons. Ryan had liked it last year when he had Miss Madison as his teacher. But Mr Moore was the death of fun. The chalk scratched on the roll-down blackboard as the pressure from each stroke sank deep into the surface.

When he wasn't scraping the chalk down the board, Mr Moore would stick out his tongue and lick it. His tongue pressed firmly to one side of the stick. The whole class would wince. He must have taught at Castle Montgomery School for a lifetime. He had taught Ryan's mum, who had hated him too, though she couldn't remember him licking chalk back then.

Cali's curly copper hair stood out against the crowd of brunettes and mostly dyed blonde hair. Not to mention his dark brown skin against the backdrop of pale faces. He and Ryan sat on a bank of desks at the back of the run-down 1970s classroom.

"I'm nearly in the top ten thousand players on Hito." Gabby tried to whisper but heads turned, showing that the whole back of the classroom had heard. "I've figured out how to get more points."

Ryan looked at Cali quizzically. Gabby's blonde locks contrasted against her sidekick counterpart's deep brunette straight strands.

"All you have to do..." Gabby looked around and then whispered a little quieter but still audibly, "...is bully people."

Tina folded her arms and looked sceptical. Her heavy fake eyelashes weighed down her eyelids, "It sounds a bit weird to rip into strangers. How will I see them cry?" They both raised their hands to their mouths to stifle their laughter.

Gabby twisted around to look at Ryan, "Are you listening to our conversation. Do you want another sandwich?" Tina and Gabby laughed again.

Ryan jumped out of his chair as he scrambled for a response, rubbing his sweaty hands on his thighs. "Erm...no Gabby. I was listening to...Mr Moore." His cheeks flushed pink. Why was he so spineless? He shouldn't take this. There was a time back in primary school that he and Gabby were friends. That seems like an eternity ago.

"Honestly, you're such a creep. No wonder you only have that one ginger mate sitting next to you."

"It's copper actually," Cali muttered.

"Silence at the back," Mr Moore stood tall and shouted, gripping his trusty chalk with one hand and holding his portly belly with the other. "Gabby, would you care to share your conversation with the whole class? It's clearly more important than learning about *Of Mice and Men*?" His deep voice ricocheted throughout the classroom.

The whole room turned around to Gabby as she blinked slowly, an acute smile growing on her tender face.

"We were saying..." she glanced over at him and smiled more vividly, "that Ryan is a geek."

The room exploded with laughter. Ryan crawled further down into his seat. A million pairs of eyes looked at him. His forehead crumpled. His eyes locked to the table. He heard Cali sighing.

"Well, that may be the case, Miss McGee, but Ryan's geekiness can't hold up our class. Onto chapter five."

The class turned back to the blackboard and Ryan buried his head in his trembling hands. When he lifted his head, he was met with the sight of Mr Moore licking the chalk once more.

The class bumbled on until break when Ryan and Cali would take their usual places in the corner of the yard. It was safest to stand here where you could see what everyone else was doing and prepare yourself for any threats that were headed your way. The most popular kids of course didn't need to do this. They knew no one would dare approach them, shout names at them, stick gum in their hair or anything else unpleasant. Therefore, they stood confidently in the centre of the yard. Gabby and Tina were among these people, as well as Gabby's boyfriend Max. He was well-known for being a nice guy, although Ryan couldn't attest to that personally. He was the captain of the school football team, and he always caught second looks from every girl.

"Something weird happened when I played Hito last night," Ryan said. "I was paired with this girl, and she managed to switch my webcam on without me knowing."

"You fell for that? Really?" Cali said. "You must have said the keywords,"

"The keywords?" Ryan raised his left eyebrow.

"Well, there's no official list of keywords. Let me guess...you said some words like 'show' and 'face.' That would have started your webcam."

"That's so creepy," Ryan's spine tingled as he remembered the incident. He pictured the webcam on his bedroom floor. "How can they get away with that?"

"Meh. They're an online game. It's unregulated. It's not like Microsoft or Nintendo. Imagine if our parents knew what they were like."

"Did you hear what Gabby said in class? Bullying gets you points, or whatever they're called. Buki?"

They both ducked as a football whooshed over their heads at the speed of a rocket and hit the door behind them.

"I hate this school," Cali said. "What were we saying? Oh yeah. For the bullying thing on Hito, I guess it could work in theory. I've never tried it. It just depends how their scoring algorithm is built."

Ryan arrived home that evening feeling relieved. Nobody could call him names or shoot a football at him here. The clock on the dining room wall read 5.45pm, Fri 13 May 2005. Its digital display jarred with the old-worldly furniture in the room. As this was Friday, the sweet sense of escape was stronger. He was not only safe for an evening, but for an entire weekend.

His mum carried a carefully crafted lasagne and put it in the middle of the table. He excitedly rushed over and took his usual seat. She scuttled off back to the kitchen. Nobody ate until everyone was at the table.

"So," Dad said, "how's your day been, son?"

"Okay," Ryan said shrugging his shoulders.

Dad looked over his head at the clock and tapped his fingers on the table. Ryan stared at the candle next to where his mum sits. The flame danced from side to side more than usual.

Mum came back into the room and Ryan and his dad stirred back into life. Ryan straightened his back as Dad pulled his chair closer to the table. She placed a bowl of overflowing salad next to the lasagne.

"You've cooked my favourite, Mum," Ryan said. "What's the special occasion?" Mum wasn't a good cook. This was the one dish that she had perfected. It was always cooked on his birthday, and sometimes instead of a cake, with candles stuffed into the melting cheese on top.

"Well, we have some news," Mum said.

All three of them dug their forks into the dish, and Dad served himself some salad from the bowl. The metal tongs clanged together. Mum chewed some lasagne. She stared down at her plate whilst Dad looked up at the clock. This news was obviously going to be bad. Why were they taking so long to say whatever it was? Thoughts rushed through his head. Was Grandma okay? Had his dad been fired?

"We...we . . ." she shovelled another chunk of lasagne into her mouth.

The tension in the air was palpable as he watched her chew and waited for the news.

"Well, you see . . . we-"

"We're separating, son," Dad interjected as he dropped his fork onto his plate. The clink echoed around the dining room. "It's just not working out."

The clock ticked five times with its digital heartbeat. Ryan's eyes became glossy. The lasagne looked less appetising now. He gazed at the portrait hanging above the fireplace of his grandmother and grandfather on their wedding day. Their love had lasted until Grandad passed away five years ago. He died holding Grandma's hand, and since that day a part of her has disappeared.

"Are you okay, Ryan?" Mum asked with her caring affectionate tone, touching his hand that rested on the table.

He turned to face her.

"I'm okay," he said as convincingly as he could. He was never good with talking about stuff.

"Let us know if you want to talk about it," she said, smiling softly. Her eyes sparkled in the candlelight.

"Donna. He said he's fine. Leave him alone. He could probably tell himself how bad things have got," Dad said, his tone chilling the room.

After dinner, Ryan went back to his attic room and turned on the PC. As usual, as soon as the desktop loaded, he scrolled with the mouse and clicked on the MSN icon. A flash of yellow at the bottom of the screen opened a chat with Cali.

Cali: *Turns out my cousins are here tonight so I'll not be around much.*

His status read offline with a greyed-out circle.

The webcam still lay in the centre of the bedroom floor. Ryan kicked it under his bed with such force he could hear it thud on the back of the wall. It could have broken but he didn't care. He needed a distraction to disappear from this heaviness: Hito. He went directly to the website. The same loading bar appeared, and he was again thrown into a waiting room with lots of strangers. "Hello, Hi, Pay" they shouted randomly. Why would someone say *pay*? Anyway, after he clicked *yes* to accept this evening's session, the American voice spoke through his speakers. He clicked a few times but there seemed to be no way to skip her.

"Welcome to Hito. You'll shortly be paired up with another hito...."

The session loaded and Ryan's hito was standing on a sandy dune. The sun was a fireball and he imagined how hot it would feel on his hito's pale skin. In the distance, golden pyramids sat on flat plains, with each brick precisely placed from the top to the very bottom. A camel with a saddle on its back strolled in front of him, completing the desert scene. He clicked the right side of the mouse and dragged the cursor around to explore the surroundings. Apart from a few cacti, and another camel wandering around in the distance, there was nothing else here.

To the left of him a transparent figure began to load. Short brown hair appeared first, followed by a freckled face and then baggy clothes, as the hito's body started to fill into life. High heels peeked out from the bottom of her flared trousers.

When she was fully loaded, Ryan typed, "Hey, asl?"

"Hey," she typed back. "14, female, Thurlcaster, you?"

Thurlcaster!?? Thurlcaster was tiny. He must know this person, especially as they were the exact same age too. He grabbed his mouse and scrolled over her character to read her username. Gabbymcgee. He blinked. It was her. Gabby from class. He scrolled over his username. Ryan2005. Ryan was a popular name; she wouldn't need to know it was him. It was time to test out her idea; that bullying earned you more buki. Now he could say what he wouldn't have dared to in class.

Chapter 3

Revenge

"Ryan, 15, Newcastle," he typed back so she couldn't guess it was him. The three dots appeared above her head. He pulled his chair closer to the screen and rested his elbow on the desk.

"Do you wear glasses in real life?" she typed.

His hand on the mouse became clammy as he looked over his hito and remembered how much it resembled him. The glasses. The polo shirt. The freckles. Would she guess it was him, even with the fake age and city?

"No, I'm not that geeky in real life," he typed.

"Haha fair. I don't look this tragic in real life either."

Phew. He'd tricked her. The plan could still go ahead.

"How are you doing anyway?" her message read.

Occasionally he liked chatting to strangers on MSN. He liked that he could be anyone he wanted. Whether that was making himself older or pretending that he was from a more exciting place, like California or the South of France. He also liked that despite lying about some elements, he could tell the truth about what he was going through and how he was feeling. They were a stranger. With his cover well assembled, now was the time for some truth.

"Not good. Terrible week at school and I just found out my parents are separating."

The three dots appeared above Gabby's head. Was she going to bully him to get more buki? He'd give her a taste of her own medicine. He could mock her for her hito's terrible baggy clothes. Or her short hair with jagged ends. In real life, she had beautiful wavy long blonde hair. He had no idea why she would choose a hito that looked nothing like her.

"Ah that's a shame. My parents divorced a few years ago. It's not a nice thing to go through. Don't blame yourself, it's not your fault."

He didn't know her parents were divorced. They seemed happy when he went round her house in primary school. He appreciated her compassion, but this didn't sound like her.

He jumped. Someone had slammed the front door, almost certainly Dad. Had they just had a big argument? Was he now gone for good? No. He remembered every Friday Dad would go to the pub with his friends. Ryan was always asleep by the time he came back so he would never hear him return.

A ping sounded through the speakers. "Let's look around this desert?" said Gabby's hito.

He accepted the invite, and they began their hike across the deserted land, walking towards the top of the sand dune.

"Did you see their separation coming?"

"Not at all. They argued but isn't that what they all do. Parents are weird."

"Hahah you're telling me! My mum nags me all the time," Gabby said.

"My mum is fine, but my dad pesters me. He thinks I should play darts just because he does."

"Darts? Boring. My mum signed me up for Pilates. Apparently, it's good for keeping your figure lean. Like I care about that. I just want to help people. Do some charity work. Try to make the world a little bit better."

He leaned back in his chair. Ryan was amazed. This really didn't sound like the super popular, self-obsessed mean girl. This was an alien. Maybe she was pretending to be someone better?

"You seem cool. Not trying too hard. Just being yourself," Gabby said. Ryan couldn't help but let out a giggle at the screen. There's no way she would say that to him if she knew he was Ryan Jones from school.

A quieter thud downstairs signalled that his mum must have also now just left the house. She had recently taken up a book club for a few hours every Friday night, which she would often bore Ryan with the details of. Telling him stories, never about the books that they've read, but about the lives of the other mothers.

Within the game they had now reached the peak and the landscape transformed before his eyes. In front of them was a mirage-like oasis. Vast lakes were dotted around the land, with palm trees, waterfalls and deer. Instead of desert, this was a green sanctuary bustling with life. It was animated beautifully; every pixel perfect.

"So, are you new?" Gabby said, "It says you've only got 100 buki. I've got a lot."

Ryan typed, ready to tell her that this was just his second session. But she'd already sent another message.

"Can you show me your face?" she said.

He froze, then pulled his hands back from the keyboard and glanced at the top of the monitor to double check that the webcam wasn't there. She was trying to trick him. Although she was wearing different stripes on the game, this was the same Gabby. The Gabby McGee who tortured him in class. His fingers stabbed the keys awkwardly. He gulped and hit enter.

"Shut up, you stupid freak. You're such a loser bragging about the amount of buki you have." He felt criminal typing this. Everything going against the core values of his personality. All his parents had taught him about how to be a good person. To treat people with respect. To be kind.

"Excuse me?" Gabby said. The three dots appeared above her head. Was she going to turn the tables and start bullying him? He was invested, there was no point stopping now. There was buki to claim. Besides, she would never know it was him. She deserved it.

"You heard me," Ryan said, "I bet in real life you're a bitch who doesn't have any friends, just suck-up followers. And come on, you're not doing charity work. You're not fooling me." He spun his computer chair around and faced his bed. Then got up and paced the length of the room a few times before daring to come back and look at the screen when he heard the next ping.

"Oh...I see what you're doing."

The adrenaline pumped through him as he typed as fast as he could. Years of things he wished he could have said. This wasn't only for him. It was for Cali too. In fact, the whole school and every underdog that had ever lived. It wasn't even exclusively about Gabby. It was for every name anyone had ever been called.

"You think you're so cool," he continued. "You're going to end up washed up with a dead-end job."

"Okay, I get it. Well done. Now you can stop."

Tears filled the corner of his eyes as the fire started to take over him. The hairs on the back of his head stood up straight. His fingers shook with every word he typed. He couldn't stop. He couldn't win a war in the yard at school, but this was a level playing field. His words were digital bullets.

"That's if you even make it until then," he typed.

"Wow, I think you're taking this a bit far..."

Tears streamed down Ryan's face as he read over the message. He wiped away his tears with a shaking hand. He paced the room, the shag carpet touching against his bare soles. He flipped open his phone and put it back down on his bed. He spun back into his chair and typed again. Ready to send out more.

"I can see why your parents couldn't stay together. They don't even want to be with you."

The three dots appeared over Gabby's hito. Would she strike back? His fingers hovered over the keys. He typed one more sentence and pressed enter before he could second guess himself.

"You'll get what's coming to you, I'll make sure of that."

The three dots disappeared from above her head. Ryan leaped up from his seat and returned to pacing the room. Rubbing his hands together as he replayed his message over and over in his head. Had he taken it too far? There was a ping. He rushed back over to the computer to see what Gabby had said. But there were no messages. Her hito was no longer there... Ryan's hito was standing on his own. The screen faded as the results loaded onto the screen.

9,600 buki earned. Position: 964,824. Increased 797,217 places.

Gabby was right about bullying people, and Ryan had got a lot of buki. But he was disgusted with himself. Ryan closed the window and went downstairs to watch a Friday night TV chat show to distract himself from what had happened. His mind occasionally flicked back to the incident and a heavy feeling settled in his stomach. He sank further into the sofa each time.

The weekend was nowhere near as relaxing as usual. Ryan's Monday dread mixed with anxiety at the thought of facing Gabby. Would she realise that the hito who looked like him was him? Would she call him out in class and embarrass him again? He'd already played the scenario through in his mind numerous times and had a script for how he would deny what he'd done. He'd say he'd been out at a restaurant on Friday with his dad. The perfect alibi. She didn't know his dad and could never ask.

Chapter 4

Missing

Everyone filed into the hall for Monday morning assembly. Teachers would make announcements and lecture them about behaviour like – too much litter on the yard – every now and then a brave student would stupidly perform a musical number to the rest of the school. Ryan couldn't imagine why anyone would put themselves in that position. But at least assembly was better than sitting in the classroom. Nothing was demanded from him in here.

There were tracks through the dust on the creaky wooden floorboards, marking the routes to the chairs. His classmates slumped in their seats as they prepared themselves to be bored. Many of the seats were empty today and he realised that it was just Year 9 in the hall. This was different. The teachers only ever held an assembly for a single year group if they had something special to discuss.

Unusually too, all of the teachers had come and lined each side of the hall with their heads facing the dusty floor. Mr Dhanial, the headteacher, entered the hall and walked between the rows of the chairs. His face looked pained, and his physique seemed smaller as he walked past the students. He stepped onto the stage as slowly as the students had dawdled in.

"We've called an assembly just for Year 9," the microphone hissed as Mr Dhanial spoke, "All other years will be told separately but we wanted to tell you all first. I'm afraid we have some bad news today..."

The room fell silent in anticipation. Everyone looked around, puzzled gazes spreading across the room like a tidal wave. Ryan looked at Cali beside him and arched his right eyebrow.

"Over the weekend one of your classmates, Gabby McGee, was reported missing."

Panicked chattering and the sound of students shuffling uncomfortably in their chairs filled the room. Ryan looked around. His own face must have been deathly white. Students were taking their phones out of their pocket as the screens lit up the hall.

"Quiet, please," said the headmaster trying to restore order in the hall. The microphone continued to hiss with every word. "We've already spoken to those of you who are closest to Gabby. This is going to be a very difficult time and we must all come together in this time of need. She was last seen on Friday evening."

Friday!? When Ryan spoke to her on Hito?

"You may see the police walking around the school, as they make enquiries and speak to teachers as well as students about Gabby. We are all devastated and just want to see her return as soon as possible."

The teachers remained standing still, sombre faces lining the hall.

"I know this is hard for you all but we all have to stick together and pray that she returns to us. The school counsellor is available at any time if you would like to go to her office and chat. The police have asked that if you have any information that may help, please let them or one of your teachers know. We've also published some new school rules and we're writing to your parents. Nobody will be able to have lunch off-site from now on. Everyone must stay in the canteen. Please do not walk home by yourself. Have a friend walk with you. Keep safe during this time."

Mr Dhanial stepped away from the mic and it hissed once more. He fled through the exit at the back of the stage whilst the teachers ushered students from the hall. Ryan rose from his chair and his knees felt heavy. He patted his forehead as his temperature soared. Why was he so nasty to her on Hito? Had he made her do something stupid?

"I wonder what's happened to her," Cali whispered. Ryan shrugged his shoulders. Cali continued, "Are you okay? It's a bit of a shock, isn't it? Even though she was a cow."

"Erm…yeah, I'm fine." Ryan rubbed his forehead again.

When he reached English class he collapsed into his seat, feeling like a tonne weight was pressing down on his chest. Neither Tina nor Max was here.

"I wonder if the police are talking to them," Cali muttered close to Ryan's ear, pointing to the empty seats. "They might think they're in on it. Maybe the police think they murdered her. Max wouldn't have done that. What do you think?"

"I don't know," Ryan replied tonelessly, continuing to stare directly forwards.

"QUIET AT THE BACK!" Mr Moore shouted. He licked the knob of chalk in his hand. The pink seemed to be his favourite.

Three single thuds knocked on the door. It sounded like the door would explode. Mr Moore stopped licking the chalk and shouted for them to come in. A police officer in his early thirties stood before the class. His uniform was pristine and the badge from his police helmet reflected the strip lights of the ceiling. Max stepped out from behind the police officer and walked over to his chair, whilst all the girls stared, drooling, which was hardly appropriate right now. Cali tutted. Tina walked behind him, her eyes fixed to the floor.

"Can Ryan Jones please come with me?" The policeman scanning the room. Ryan felt sick. He gripped the legs of the chair.

"Go on Ryan, follow the policeman," Mr Moore shouted as he held his belly. "Don't keep him waiting." Ryan got up and sheepishly walked towards the door.

Building Zero was the staff and admin block. No pupils came here except for prefects and troublemakers who were sent to the headteacher's office. The policeman marched him to a room where he took a seat behind the desk alongside a young female officer. A smile was pinned to her face, and she stared directly into Ryan's eyes as he took a seat opposite them both.

Ryan sat straight in the chair, trying not to let his body language give any clues as to what was going on inside of his head. A single light swung above his head, like a spotlight in an interrogation room. This felt like an interview room, not a school office.

"Hi, Ryan. I'm DCI Binyon," she said as she shuffled papers on the desk. The police officer next to her coughed. "Oh, and this is PC Gables." He brought his hand from his mouth and poised a fountain pen above a clean pad of paper.

"So, this is new for me. This whole DCI thing," she muttered, "but I am set on solving my first ever case. And I think you can help me. Ryan, I'm guessing you know why you're here. Your classmate Gabby has gone missing."

"Yes, I heard in assembly today," he sheepishly replied. He couldn't look around without looking very suspicious. "Shouldn't my parents be here with me?"

"Oh, you're not a suspect! Don't worry about that. It's far too early to assert who the suspects are. Or if there are any suspects. Maybe she's just gone on a mini break without telling anyone."

PC Gables tutted and interrupted, "We're just trying to garner as much information as possible. Then we can determine what we need to do. Did you know Gabby well?"

"No," Ryan replied defensively, "She was in a couple of my classes but that's all. It's scary to hear that she's gone missing. They said in assembly it was Friday night? Any idea where she went to?" He leaned forward eager to hear more.

"It was indeed Friday. We wanted to speak to you, Ryan..." her eyes grew as she placed her elbows on the desk, "because Gabby has been playing an online game called Hito. Have you heard of it?"

Ryan gulped. Were they onto him? She also wrongly pronounced the game, at least wrongly to him. She said it as *High-to*, instead of *Hee-toe*.

"I've heard of it." He was focused on a small crack in the middle of the window between the police officers' heads.

"We've contacted Hito to get more information on her movements within the game. They haven't been the most cooperative, but they have given us some information." She eventually pulled out a sheet from the pile of papers. She picked up her glasses and placed them crookedly on her face. "They told us that the last person she talked to on there had the username..." she held the paper inches from her eyes, "Ryan2005."

He gulped.

Chapter 5

Investigation

His nostrils flared. He shuffled his hands before gripping the legs of his chair until his knuckles turned white.

"Do...do you think that's me? Is that why I'm here?" he asked with a quiver in his voice.

"Well, Ryan," she looked straight into his eyes, "we know that users on the game are more likely to be connected with people who are geographically closer to them. So, we're speaking to all pupils named Ryan in this school to see if we can identify Ryan2005."

Ryan looked down at his lobster-red palms, sore from rubbing them on his trousers.

"I don't play Hito, sorry," he muttered still looking down. He pressed his hands together and could feel the warmth of his lies flowing through. He willed the floor to swallow him whole.

"Do you have any other information that might help us?" she said, "Or anything really. Any other Ryans you think it could be? Or anybody nicknamed Ryan? Or anything weird you know about the game? Gosh there's a lot I need to work on. Sorry this case really came out the blue."

PC Gables tutted whilst hovering his pen over the notepad.

"No," Ryan said.

As she attempted to shuffle the papers, she accidentally dropped them to the floor. After gathering them up, she took a deep breath. "So, we're asking everyone this. How do I put it...well...well, it's important, well..."

PC Gables interrupted. "Where were you on Friday evening between the hours of 8pm and 11pm?" Ryan could feel the heat from the spotlight on his now reddening face.

"I was in the house."

"And can your parents confirm that?"

"Not exactly," he stumbled, "My mum was at a book club and my dad was at the pub. I promise you I was in the house." PC Gables scribbled something onto the paper with the fountain pen.

"Well, thank you for speaking to us. If we need to speak to you again, we'll let you know." DCI Binyon stood up and gestured towards the door. Ryan nodded to them both and left the room before they had the chance to ask anything else.

He raced down the corridor and threw open the door of the boys' toilets. Standing at the sink, he splashed water onto his face. The cold water soothed him. He lifted his head and stared into the mirror. "Did I do this?"

Hito might give the police the email address for the Ryan2005 account. What would stop them from releasing his conversation with Gabby to the police and then he would no doubt be the number one suspect. He replayed his last message to Gabby over in his mind. "You'll get what's coming to you, I'll make sure of that."

He needed to find out what had happened to Gabby. To clear his name but also to clear his conscience.

His stomach turned. He stood before the mirror and the sensation grew. It was approaching the top of his throat. He ran into a cubicle, locked the door with fumbling hands and crouched over the toilet. Sick hit the bowl, splattering all over the sides. Sitting there, tears appeared in the corners of his eyes. This was overwhelming. There was too much to think about. He heard footsteps out in the bathroom. Someone was now in here. He lifted his head and tried to slow down his breathing, so they didn't hear him. Then the main door shot open again and the sound of a tile cracking from the impact boomed in the echoey bathroom.

"Get out the boys toilet!" a male voice said.

"No. We need to talk about it," a girl replied.

Ryan knew these voices. It was Max and Tina. He squatted without moving a muscle. Would they notice the locked cubicle he was hiding in? His fingertips resting on the side of the toilet basin and his legs ached from crouching.

"I'm not chatting about anything. It's not the right time," Max said, "What if someone hears? Leave me alone."

"You can't run forever. It's killing me not talking about it," Tina said. The door slammed again. He heard Max presumably pull down his zip and use the urinal, before washing his hands and also leaving the room. Did they know something more about Gabby's disappearance? What didn't Max want to talk about?

When he was gone, Ryan went back to Mr Moore's class. Everyone turned their heads and whispered as he slumped back to his desk. He glanced over at Tina and Max who were sitting there in silence, both facing the front of the room. Mr Moore had his back to everyone, writing something that made no sense onto the blackboard. Each word he wrote, he paused to lick his chalk.

At break, Ryan and Cali sat in the canteen whilst Cali ate an apple. The sea-blue plastic chairs and the sand-coloured tables made the room look like a sad beach. A resort that you didn't want to visit.

Every word tasting like sick, Ryan told Cali everything that had happened. How he bullied Gabby on

Hito the night she went missing and threatened to hurt her. The police interrogation and how the police knew the username of the account she last spoke to. The confrontation between Max and Tina in the boys' toilet. It all came out like word vomit.

"Wow," Cali said as he stared at the sand-coloured table, "it's not like you to say that stuff to Gabby. You must have been really mad!"

Ryan despairingly nodded.

"I need to find out what's happened to her. Will you help me?"

"Okay, I'll help you investigate. I know you didn't mean it. But we need to find more info before the police find anything out. We need to identify our key suspects. You said her parents are separated? They should be our first suspects."

"Why's that?" Ryan said looking perplexed.

"Have you never seen a crime show? It's always a relative of the victim. We need to know if they had a motive, or some crazy past that has led them to do this."

"Hmmm, true. We'll have to think how we find out more about them. Whoever's behind Hito is a suspect too. We know she played it the night she went missing. She was good at it so she must have played it a lot. And what weird game creators allow your webcam to be switched on without you knowing?" Ryan shivered a moment, until he remembered that his webcam was safely tucked away under his bed. "Do you know any other tricks on Hito? Aside from the webcam hack. Anything that can get us to know it more?"

Cali shook his head as he chewed his apple. "The point of the game is that you find stuff out as you play! You'll just ruin the game for yourself."

"Cali," Ryan said sternly, "I'm not going to play this game for fun. We need to have it as part of the investigation. Spoil it for me. There might be some useful information."

Cali sighed, then proceeded to list what he'd found, whilst Ryan absorbed every word.

1. The weird chatroom at the start shows all the possible matches for the connection session. No buki can be earned in the chatroom so nobody takes it too seriously. If you see someone in the chatroom that you want to be connected to, press CTRL + 7 and then type their username into the bar.
2. Although the game limits each user to just one connection session every day, you can trick the game into allowing you to have another session by switching to a private browser.
3. Whilst in the session, if you type "gift buki" and then enter a number, you can gift any amount of buki you wish to the other player.

Chapter 6

Stakeout

Ryan grabbed his flip phone out of his pocket to check the time. Five minutes left of break.

"And what about the police telling me that you're more likely to get paired with someone who lives near you?" He tapped his fingers on the table.

"Oh god, yeah," Cali put down the apple core, "in fact I don't think there's any chance of getting paired with anyone outside of Thurlcaster. Everyone just lies about their location to stay anonymous." Ryan wormed in his chair thinking about how the girl who tricked him with his webcam must be someone in school.

"So, we need to investigate Gabby's parents. Hito. And also Tina and Max," Ryan said pulling himself together. He leaned back as a group of students walked past the table, trying to look as casual as possible.

"Tina should definitely be a suspect," Cali muttered under his breath as another group passed, "So that's our list of suspects. Gabby's parents. The game. And Tina-"

"What about Max? He's Gabby's boyfriend. He has got to be a suspect. And I heard him and Tina arguing in the toilets? They could be hiding something together."

Cali looked out across the canteen. "I don't think so. He doesn't strike me as a kidnapper." Cali crossed his arms. The smell of a cheese and ham panini drifted through the air.

Ryan laughed. "You don't even know him. We can't rule him out yet." He checked his phone. The bell would be ringing for the next lesson in just a few seconds.

"Fine," Cali sighed, "but we should leave him last to investigate. Saves us from wasting our time. We have more likely suspects."

The two of them headed out of the canteen and to their art lesson.

When Ryan got home that night, he was greeted by crying coming from the living room.

"Have you heard the news, son!?" Mum said as he cautiously entered. She wailed as she tucked herself into the sofa, pulling a blanket over her bare legs. "Gabby has gone missing." She sniffled as she rubbed her nose.

He felt sorry for her. She was like an emotional sponge and always took on everyone else's problems. Dad would often say that she needed a full-time job, rather than her part-time cleaning one, to keep her mind occupied.

Ryan sat down on a stool.

"Gabby's mum Lorraine is in my book club. I've never liked Lorraine, but I can't imagine how horrible it must be to have...have..." She stopped herself with another wail, "your child missing." She tucked her face into the blanket and Ryan could just about make out what she said, "I hope nobody has snatched her." She rubbed her tears and runny nose onto the blanket.

"What about Gabby's dad?"

Mum lifted her head up. "He's dead. They separated before he died. Lung cancer a few years ago." Her eyes streamed with more tears.

Gabby hadn't mentioned that her dad had died. He thought about the happy family setting he used to see when he visited their house as a kid.

"Mum, was Lorraine at book club on Friday when Gabby went missing?"

"She wasn't. A bit strange. That's the first time she's missed it since I've been there," her crying suffocated the blanket. Ryan got up and walked over to his mum and nested next to her on the sofa. He threw his arms around her. She continued to cry whilst he comforted her, occasionally dropping in a reassuring message about how he is sure everything will be okay. He hoped himself they would be okay.

Her tears ran out and he made his way up to his bedroom after hugging her once more. Powering on the PC, he gazed out the window whilst it booted up. Lorraine was a key suspect to investigate.

Ryan went to the Hito website. His profile name Ryan2005 stared back at him. This account wasn't safe. The police knew about it. He couldn't risk using it. He scrolled down and logged out. It took him only five minutes to create an email address, one with a fake name. Then he went back to the Hito website and created a new account with fake details. There was now nothing identifiable that matched Ryan, bar the fact both this character and him were male. Timothybrown was his new username.

A flash of yellow popped up at the bottom of the screen and he clicked, expecting to see an MSN message from Cali. What? Who was this? This person wasn't on his contact list. Their name read "Thurl123." There was no profile picture either. Only an icon where one should be.

Thurl123: *I saw you being escorted out of class today to be questioned by the police. If you know anything about what happened, keep it to yourself. Life isn't always good to those that open their mouths, and I can guarantee that if you say something you shouldn't, you'll regret it. You have been warned. Don't try messaging back, I won't respond.*

Ryan froze in fear as he sat re-reading the message. He raised his hand that was quivering from his lap and scrolled over the name. He right-clicked to save it as a contact and switched off the monitor. The room fell into darkness. He went over and lay on his bed, without turning on the light, preferring to stay in the blanketed darkness. Every person in his class was now a suspect. Anyone who could have known he was escorted out. Downstairs, a few whimpers rose through the house from Mum now in her bedroom. This wasn't going to be a restful night for anyone. He drifted off into an uncomfortable sleep.

He was exhausted the next day and just wanted to lie in bed after school, but there were more pressing matters.

"You're late." Ryan looked down at his watch. Cali let out a pant and gripped his hips. It took a few moments until he could stand up straight. He explained how he ran from his house after being held up at dinner.

"Which one is it?" Cali looked at the street of identical terraced houses. Ryan pointed to a red door in the middle of the street. He'd seen the house on the local news continually that week, which streamed a segment of CCTV footage of Gabby walking down Devon's Road at 10.24pm in a fur coat and a pair of Ugg boots. A surprising outfit choice considering it was May. The voiceover would say how there was no more footage of her after that time, then the camera would return to the presenter with the red door in the background. The same red door he often went through to play with Gabby when he was growing up.

A few film crews were dotted along the street, and a policeman was standing at Lorraine's door. The officer kept his eyes on the half-dozen bystanders, including Ryan and Cali. They walked back to the top of the street and hid behind a parked car.

"Well...what's the plan?" Cali said.

"This is it. We just need to watch Lorraine's house," Ryan whispered needlessly. Cali rolled his eyes. "Have you never seen a spy movie? They always do a stake out and they always find some clues."

"Sure, and what do we expect to see? Lorraine dragging Gabby's dead body out of the house in front of the news cameras?"

Ryan gazed at the red door through the windows of the car. When it got dark, the news crews packed up their kit and drove away. The policeman remained at the door, his eyes still fixed on any approaching movement as he surveyed the street. Nothing was going to get past him.

A light flicked on upstairs in the house, illuminating the policeman's face. Both he and Cali peered up at the lit window, still crouching from behind the car. Lorraine was walking around her bedroom. She picked something up from the dressing table and tugged at her ears. She was putting in earrings. The light went off and then another light switched on. This time a frosted glass pane prevented them from seeing what was happening. The boys glanced at each other. Trying to see into a bathroom was weird, even though the frosted glass did its job well.

A car with tinted windows swerved around a corner and screeched to a halt outside the red door. The police officer squinted and walked a few paces forward with his hand firmly placed on his holster. Ryan and Cali let out a collective gasp; this was the first time they noticed that the policeman had a gun. Thurlcaster was far too small to ever see this. What were they expecting to happen? The red door swung open as Lorraine stepped out in a black dress, her sparkling earrings drooping down resting on her shoulders. She tapped the policeman on the arm and then trotted to the car before getting in. The car drove off as fast as it had arrived. Ryan and Cali leaped up from their feet and ran after it. They saw the car taking the next left and chased, wheezing and grunting. They turned the corner and saw it turn right. They ran as fast as they could, Ryan gaining a better lead than Cali. Then Ryan took a right turn, but the car was gone. They'd lost it.

Cali came running up to Ryan, wheezing heavily.

"Well, I think we might have to improve our fitness before we do our next stakeout," he panted.

"Where the hell is she off to?" Ryan said as he gazed at the now empty street. "Did you see who was with her in the car?" Cali shook his head.

Chapter 7

Book Club

As the week went on, more police officers appeared at the school. One stood at the entrance gates and made eye contact with each pupil as they walked in. He towered over the students. Thankfully he didn't have a gun. Ryan tried to avoid his eyes; it was like his stare could penetrate Ryan's mind and read his thoughts.

In the school canteen, a policewoman would circle the room and ask pupils at different tables if they had ever spoken to Gabby. She would often circle back to the same tables and ask the same question, presumably to see if she would get a different response. Or she was just very forgetful.

Posters were put up all around Thurlcaster asking anyone with information to come forward. An anonymous hotline had been set up to provide tips to the police, and Gabby's mother, Lorraine, was personally offering a £10,000 reward for any information that led to her daughter being found.

"Ryan, I'm heading out. Can you lock the door?" Mum shouted from the hallway. Ryan raced down the metal ladder from the attic. He passed his old box room, before he had moved into the newly refurbished attic and appeared at the top of the narrow stairs.

"Where are you going?"

"To book club. You know I go there every Friday. We're holding it at Lorraine's house tonight." She paused and smiled sympathetically. "She's struggling so she wants us all there to distract her."

Ryan jogged down the stairs towards his mum. "Let me take you there. I need some fresh air." He grabbed his coat from the banister and threw it onto his shoulders in one swift movement.

The two of them set off on the ten-minute walk to Lorraine's house. Mum talked the entire way: asking him if he thought she should have bought a gift for Lorraine, repeating how she didn't like her but felt sorry for her. He had no idea where this unjust dislike of Lorraine had come from. Ryan really wanted to chat about the separation, but he could tell that his mother wanted to talk about anything but that right now. He listened to their shoes on the cobbles, and watched the streetlights that were switching on one at a time.

They arrived at the door and the policeman stepped aside. Mum rapped three times with the knocker until a light came on. Lorraine opened the door. She had big dark circles under her eyes, her hair was unkempt, and she was wearing a pink t-shirt and baggy pyjama bottoms: the total opposite to how glamourous she looked when Ryan had saw her skipping out the house the other night.

"Thanks for coming. I really appreciate it."

"Of course. I can't imagine what you must be going through love," Mum said as she clasped her hands.

"Come on in, a few people are already here," Lorraine said.

As Mum stepped into the hall, Ryan tapped her shoulder. "Sorry, I'm desperate for the toilet. Is it okay if I use it before I head back home?"

The policeman glared at Ryan.

"Um . . . of course." Lorraine had caught the conversation. "It's just upstairs. The furthest door on the left. In fact, you probably remember anyway."

Mum and Lorraine disappeared into the room at the end of the hallway, switching off the light behind them as Ryan climbed the stairs. On his way up, the streetlight shone onto the stairs, and he saw family photos adorning every inch of the wall. Gabby at lots of different ages. A photo of them holidaying when she was young. Christmases. Birthdays. He saw a picture of him and Gabby at a play area. He remembered the day well. And then photos began to show only her mum and her. These he hadn't seen before.

When he reached the top, in front of him stood a door with tape reading 'POLICE LINE DO NOT CROSS.' It was Gabby's room. He was scared to open it. The more he stared at it however, the less scary it became. What lay on the other side? His hand hovered over the handle as if the door might open without him having to turn the knob. Mustering the courage, he turned it and ducked under the tape.

The room lay in complete darkness. He switched on the light and was greeted by a sea of pink and florals. The duvet, curtains and walls were all pink, with floral touches on the fluffy rug and cushions. A poster of Justin Timberlake hung on the wall opposite the bed. Artwork with her signature covered part of the wall. She was a magnificent painter. He had no idea that she liked art as much as him. Admittedly she was a lot better.

Gabby's room would likely hold some secrets as to her whereabouts. Of course, the tape on the door must mean that the police have already taken any evidence back to the station. He had one thing they didn't have, however: the mind of a teenager. Teenagers always have something they want to hide from their parents, or the police, and he was sure that Gabby would be no different.

He dropped to the floor and stuck his head under the bed. The dust puffed up as he began moving things around. A tennis racket. A Barbie doll. A microphone

with a karaoke unit. He pulled out a brown card-
board box and flipped open the lid. The box had no
dust on the top of it, as if it had already been examined recently. Inside lay various documents. He flicked
through them one by one. 100% attendance in Year 7
award. Exam results from Year 8. Straight 'A's across
the board; she had always been very clever. 50 metre
swimming award. A letter lay hidden at the bottom
of the box, signed by the headteacher, Mr Dhanial. It
was handwritten and thanked Gabby for her support
in raising money for the children of a school in Ghana.
So, she was telling the truth about wanting to help
others and do charity work. Maybe her Hito self was
her real self.

"Ryan!" a voice shouted, "Are you okay up there?"

Ryan panicked and threw the box back under the
bed. "Yes, Mum, just in the bathroom." Her voice must
have come from the bottom of the stairs. Footsteps
walked back along the hallway and away from him. He
needed to find some useful information fast. Gabby's
house was the same layout as his, and she had the
equivalent of the room he'd occupied when he was
younger, before he was able to move up to the attic.

Peering into the space above the oak wardrobe, he
saw a vent. He used to hide things in the same vent
at home. He grabbed the pink chair from Gabby's desk
and gently placed it in front of the wardrobe, making
as little noise as possible. He grabbed his keys out of

his pocket and used them to turn the screws. Holding the screws in his hand, he flipped up the vent.

This was going to be it. The answer to all his questions. He willed there to be a map inside with a path to Gabby's whereabouts. But his thoughts stopped dancing when he found nothing but darkness.

He stretched his arm inside until his hand hit the back of the vent and clunked on the metal wall. Nothing. He sighed in exasperation. As he was pulling out, something furry brushed against him.

"What the hell?"

Chapter 8

Diary

He yanked his arm out in horror and the cover smashed shut. Was it a rat? A wave of courage flooded through him, and he lifted the vent again. There was no animal to be seen. No scurrying to be heard.

When he stroked the ceiling of the vent, he realised something was attached to it. Sticky tape secured the object to the top of the vent. He pulled it as hard as he could, nearly stumbling off the chair as he did.

He got down and looked at the pink furry book that was in his hands. "2005 Diary" the cover read. He glanced through it and saw that lots of the entries had been torn out leaving only jagged teeth of paper. Only a few complete entries remained.

He screwed the vent back in place, put the chair back on the other side of the room and ducked back under the police tape with the diary in hand. He went to the bathroom, flushed the chain, then went downstairs. Shouting a quick goodbye through the kitchen wall, he tucked the book under his jacket and strutted past the policeman out into the now fully lit street.

He made his way up the metal ladder to his room, panting for breath. He'd run all the way home, not even stopping at crossings for the green man to come on. He jumped onto his bed, shoes still on, and stared at the diary in his hands. He wiped the steam from his glasses and started turning the remaining intact pages.

Thursday 28th April 2005

Dear diary,

I had an awful day at school. Tina and I got into a fight and now she isn't talking to me. It was so awkward having to sit next to her in lessons, trying not to look at her. The fight started because I said I wouldn't be able to come to her birthday at the end of May because I'm going to do another piano recital for a charity night. This time it's to raise money for the animal rescue shelter. I owe them considering the amazing years I had with Buster. She thinks I'm being selfish and should put her first.

Maybe she is right. I am her best friend. I've been crying since I got back home. She texted me saying she never wants to speak to me again. She said she'll get revenge if I decide not to come. I'm not much of a birthday person, so if she decides to never come to another birthday of mine, I won't care. But I don't want her to be upset. I hope we manage to work things out. I just want to play Hito to take my mind off this.

Gabby xoxo

Thursday 5th May 2005

Dear diary,

I don't feel like I belong. I feel like my life is pretend and I just act a certain way to please others. The stupid names I call people. I think I only do it because others around me laugh and now expect it. How can I tell them that I'm a fraud? A fraud who doesn't really belong. I think that's why I like playing Hito. I can be my true self there. No preconceptions from anyone, just Gabby. Maybe one day it'll be enough to just be me, but there's no chance of that at school. After year 11, I'll go to a different college, and I promise I'll be me. A new start. I only have two years to wait.

Gabby xoxo

P.s. Tino6000 is still giving me a lot of buki. I'm going up the leaderboard super-fast!

Thursday 12th May 2005

Dear diary,

It's 10.30pm and I'm sitting as usual at my desk. Tina seems to finally understand why I can't come to her birthday. There's something that feels very off about her recently, though. I look at her and sometimes think I actually don't know her at all. It's mine and Max's one-year anniversary this Sunday. There's not much to cele-brate. He stopped kissing me months ago. The most I can *look forward to these days is a hug. There's no point in us still going out, we may as well break up. When I said this to him last week, he started telling me how much he loves me and needs me in his life. He even cried! I like it when he tells me I'm wanted. I just wish that he would make me feel wanted with his words, rather than waiting for me to threaten breaking up with him. He is very handsome, and everyone constantly tells me what a good couple we are, but why can't I see for myself this good couple that everyone talks about? Also – my mum LOVES him. She has her own man to focus on so she should keep her head out of my personal life lol. I don't make any comments on her man, and if I did it wouldn't be nice – he obviously hates me. No one will replace Dad. Urgh life is so hard. Only a few years until my life can start properly and I can be free.*

Gabby xoxo

That was the last entry in the diary. She went missing the next day.

Gabby was different from what Ryan had thought; better than what he had thought. It was refreshing to see that she felt like him; that neither of them was living the life they wanted right now. Outsiders.

He leaped off the bed, leaving the diary on his bed and logged onto his PC. He clicked the MSN icon and saw that Cali was online.

Ryan: *Huge News! I found a way into her house and found her diary.*

Cali: *Amazing! And what does it say? Any more suspects?*

Ryan: *Her mum should be a suspect as we thought. She's been dating a new man that hates Gabby. We need more on her mum and whoever this guy is. There's a Tino6000 on Hito too who was supplying Gabby with buki. Seems a bit odd to be gifting someone so much buki without any clear reason. Also, Tina and she had a bit of a rocky friendship. And she tried to break up with Max.*

Cali: *Okay, lots to go on! Let's focus on Gabby's mum and then look at the rest. This Thurl123 who messaged you on MSN must be scared of us finding out more. Are they online?*

Ryan glanced at the list of online contacts on the right-hand side of the screen. No sign of Thurl123.

Chapter 9

Chocolates

The bell above the shop rang as Ryan walked through. Patrick greeted him with a friendly smile as he walked past the counter and headed for the far aisle, nodding on his way past. He stood at the centre of the aisle and scanned the shelf of confectionery for something suitable. Anything over £10 would be too expensive to afford. Anything below £5 would be an insult. He was relieved when his eyes finally landed on a box of Finty's luxury chocolates for £8. Perfect.

As he left the shop his phone vibrated. He flipped it open and read the SMS. It was from Cali.

"Sorry, I can't make it anymore. My cousins have come around last minute."

Ryan would have to do this mission alone, without the Robin to his Batman. They'd planned earlier to find out where Lorraine was last Friday evening when Gabby went missing. They would go to Lorraine's house and ask her a few questions, very subtly of course, about where she'd been.

If she didn't have a clear alibi, they would continue to investigate her surreptitiously. Hide outside her house and see where she went. Look through her bins for suspicious transactions on bank statements. Nothing would be off limits. Lorraine was suspect number one. Ryan felt awful suspecting that a mother could be the cause of her child's disappearance, but it made sense. Especially after reading her diary.

He reached the top of Lorraine's street and dawdled towards the red door. This was going to be hard by himself. His heart was thumping as if it would jump out of his chest at any moment. He couldn't come across too rude. After all, he wasn't entitled to know where she was when Gabby went missing. What if Lorraine slammed the door in his face and rang his mum?

He knocked once then turned away, ready to abandon the mission, hoping that no one was home. The creak of the door opening made him turn back around.

"Ryan," Lorraine said, pulling her dressing gown tightly around her, "What are you doing here?"

"I..." he said, shuffling the box of chocolates in his hands, "I just wanted to check that you're doing okay. It must be awful what you're going through."

"Thanks," her legs crossed as she stood there, "I appreciate that." Her hand disappeared behind the door, "Well, thanks for-."

"We all miss Gabby at school," he muttered, staring at the ground.

Lorraine's hand still behind the door, ready to close it. "Hopefully we'll find her soon. I really appreciate you coming around." She moved to close the door again.

"I got these for you," he said, holding the box of chocolates up.

"Thanks, that's really kind of you." She inched the door slightly open and grabbed the box from his hand.

"I had to speak to the police," Ryan stepped forward, clearly ignoring the social cues to leave. "They said they were talking to everyone at school. I was just wondering if there's anything they might be missing. Do you know what time she headed out that night?"

"I'm not sure. I wasn't home so I don't know what time she left," Lorraine said as she raised her eyebrows.

"Oh, right," he muttered, "and where were you, if you don't mind me asking?" He didn't dare look at her face and instead focused on the ground. He could see her feet entwined in each other.

"Who's that, Lorraine?" a male voice shouted from inside the house.

"I think it's best you go now," she gasped, flustered.

Ryan recognised the man's voice. He took in a deep breath as his dad emerged from the living room and stood next to Lorraine. Their eyes met and she smiled gently at Dad, wrapping her arm around his waist. This wasn't right. His dad was with another woman. Someone who wasn't his mum. Ryan didn't want to look at them. He stared very obviously at the house next door instead. Silence descended on all three of them.

"I think it's time I told you something," Dad said, grabbing his coat. "Lorraine, I'll be back in 20 minutes." He closed the door behind him. Ryan still avoiding any eye contact.

They paused for a second before Dad led the way out of the garden. Ryan walked behind him reluctantly.

"This isn't how I wanted to tell you, son." He stepped back to walk alongside Ryan.

"Tell me what, exactly?"

"Well, come on." Dad laughed, fidgeting with his hands, "I'm sure you can guess. Well, I'm with Lorraine."

"I could see that," Ryan said, fiddling with the cuffs on his jacket. "So, you cheated on Mum and that's why you are separating? You left that part out the story."

"No!" Dad's voice rose, "I would never do that to your mother. Parents don't tell their children everything, you know, Ryan. Some things kids just can't understand."

"I'm fourteen, I think I know what an affair is," Ryan said sarcastically.

"How dare you! Lorraine was never an affair," Dad said. He stopped walking and rubbed his forehead. He took a deep breath. "Look, I know this must be hard, and believe me I didn't want you finding out like this. But you have found out. And now we can all start to move on and process things. This isn't a secret to your mum."

"Okay," Ryan said, "So that's it. It's out. Now you don't have to worry about telling me. Well, what about me? I only just found out you and Mum were splitting up and now this."

"Look, I'm sorry for raising my voice. I know this must be hard for you. I'm sorry how you found out. Me and your mum have been struggling for the past few years. I met Lorraine at the start of this year, and we hit it off straight away. Your mum has known since the start. We just were waiting for the right time to tell you. We wanted to ease you into it rather than me suddenly moving out."

"You're moving out!? I thought we'd all still live to-gether," Ryan exclaimed, his eyes widening.

"I am moving out. We were going to tell you about Lorraine at the start of June once you felt more settled about the separation news. Then obviously all of this happened with Gabby. Lorraine needs me right now, son. I dread to think how she must feel. I can't imagine how it would be if you just disappeared into thin air."

"Did you know her well, Dad?" Ryan probed. He remembered how Gabby's diary had talked about how she didn't like her mother's new man. Was his dad part of it?

"Well, I only met her a few times really. I feel very sorry about the whole situation, though."

"Why do you feel sorry? You didn't do it. Or is there something else you're not telling me?" Ryan snarked.

"Don't be so stupid!" Dad's voice raised. "I guess I just didn't get a chance to know her. She was always playing that bloody game Hito. And if I hadn't suggested to Lorraine to go out for a meal, then we would have been in the house and would have stopped Gabby from leaving so late..."

"You were with Lorraine!? I thought you were at the pub? You go there every Friday, when Mum's at her book club."

"Well, not that Friday. Of all Fridays, why did I decide to take her out then? I'll never forgive myself."

"Well, at least we know one thing... Lorraine didn't do it if she was with you."

"You're joking, surely." Dad said frowning.

"Sorry, a badly timed joke," he lied, "One more question, Dad. Did Gabby know about you and Lorraine?' He stopped walking and stared at his dad.

"Well...well...well, that's not really relevant, is it? Maybe Lorraine told her at some point."

"Okay, I guess it wouldn't be fair if Gabby had known but I hadn't. That's all," Ryan said, as he walked ahead, satisfied with the outcome of his questioning. The diary had already confirmed to him that Gabby had known about their relationship.

The thought of seeing Gabby at school, and her knowing more about his parents' relationship made him feel sick. It annoyed him. She could have told Max and Tina. And God knows who else. How many people at school had known his dad was seeing Lorraine before he found out?

When they got home Ryan headed straight up to the attic, whilst Dad headed back out to Lorraine's. Mum came up and offered to speak to Ryan about Lorraine and his dad, but he didn't want to. He needed to process this. He had barely thought that much about his parents separating because of Gabby's disappearance. Now he would need to process that his dad was dating the victim's mother. As Gabby wisely said, he only had a couple of years until his life started. Then he could be out of here.

Chapter 10

Rainforest

Breakfast the next day crawled around. Mum made pancakes. Dad had joined them, and Ryan now thought how easy it must have been for his dad to only appear at mealtimes, and then go and see Lorraine without raising any suspicion.

"Are you sure you're, okay?" Mum asked as she put the plate of pancakes in front of him, facing away from Dad.

"Not really," he said, picking up his fork. "I feel like you both hid so much from me."

She didn't respond so he looked up from the maple sauce dripping down the pancakes and saw that she had a single tear in the corner of her left eye. Her face still shielded from Dad.

"Mum?" he asked, "are you okay?"

"It's okay, Ryan. We're sorry for not telling you. We should have. Now you enjoy your pancakes," she said. She walked back into the kitchen. Dad seemed oblivious to Mum's distress.

There were no plans for today so after he'd filled up on pancakes, Ryan headed upstairs and opened MSN on the computer. Before he could open the window and type a message, Cali had already sent one through.

Cali: *How did seeing Lorraine go? Did you get anything from her on where she was?*

Ryan: *I did. Turns out she has a watertight alibi.*

Cali: *What did she say? Who's her alibi with? We need to plan our next suspect interrogation. Sorry again I couldn't make it yesterday.*

Ryan: *This new guy she's dating. She was with him on Friday. Tino6000 or Tina maybe should be our next suspect.*

Cali: *New guy? Do you know who it is?*

Ryan: *No. I wonder if Tino6000 and Tina are the same person. Very similar name-wise.*

Cali: *Could be. Remember how I said if someone is in the chatroom, you can cheat the system and force Hito to make your connection session with them? Maybe for Tino6000 we need to wait them out on Hito.*

Ryan: *Sounds like a plan. And what about Tina?*

Cali: *Oh, Tina will be easy. She's having her birthday party on Thursday. We can just go there and see if we can find anything out.*

Ryan: *I'm not invited though, are you?*

Cali: *I got invited by a friend of a friend. You wouldn't know them. Anyway, it seems like an open thing so you should be fine to come along.*

In the afternoon, Ryan spent more time on Hito. Waiting in the chatroom to see if Tino6000 would drop in so he could get some more information from them. They didn't turn up, so a couple of times Ryan allowed the system to drop him into a connection session with a stranger, using the trick of going into a private browsing session so Hito didn't limit him to one connection session per day.

Ryan found himself in a rainforest. Foliage hung down all around him. A boa constrictor slithered past his legs, whilst tarantulas creeped up the trees. A group of spider monkeys circled high above. Through the blanketed rain he could just about make out a treehouse. He fumbled the mouse to change his viewpoint and made his way up there. He ascended the ladder screwed into the trunk. When he reached the top, he walked across the planked terrace complete with a hammock and a BBQ.

The treehouse was huge on the inside, much bigger than it appeared from outside, at least half the size of a football pitch. There was a fire burning on the far left of the room, a huge TV mounted on the wall and a bear skin rug covering the middle of the floor.

"Hello." Another hito appeared from the door opposite him. "I'm guessing you're from Castle Montgomery school? Or are you going to pretend to be from somewhere else too?"

Ryan laughed reading the message on the screen. "I guess I won't, no," he typed back.

The hito walked closer to Ryan, her jungle-themed outfit reminded him of Jane from Tarzan. Her purple hair was unique.

"You don't know who I am, I don't know who you are, but we know we probably pass each other in real life. Strange hey?"

"I guess it is," he typed back, thinking how peculiar this game was.

"I guess it won't make a difference if I do this, then." She walked closer to Ryan and kissed him.

Ryan had never actually been kissed. He imagined how it must feel for his hito. To feel the girl's skin push against his. The body heat radiating from her as he wrapped his arms around her. Moving her hair away from her face and then holding onto her head. He pulled himself closer to the screen. He scrolled his cursor over her hito, and a range of options popped up. Kiss. Punch. Smell. Lift up. Hug. He clicked the kiss option and returned the favour. He liked the thrill of knowing this was someone who went to his school. Maybe they'd want to kiss him in real life too.

After a few more kissing exchanges, Ryan's hito went and stood next to the fire.

"Well, that was interesting," he typed, "I hope you don't turn out to be a guy."

"Or even worse," she typed with the three dots appearing above her head, "I could be a teacher..."

"What?" he typed back.

"Haven't you heard? Apparently, there's a teacher at Castle Montgomery who comes onto here and chats to kids. Weird or what?"

Ryan pulled his wheeled office chair closer to the screen as he re-read her message. A rotating rolodex appeared in Ryan's mind. Each card with the image and name of a teacher at the school. He flicked through each card. It could be any of them. There were too many. It was an impossible game of Guess Who.

He wrote out three different messages and then settled for, "any idea on who it could be?"

The three dots lit up above the other hito. "No idea, but I'd put money on Mr Roberts. He always gives me the creeps." Ryan's rolodex flicked to Mr Roberts' card. He was young, in his early twenties. He seemed to get on so well with the students, but would he spend his time after school chatting on here?

"Promise you're not a teacher?" she said.

"I promise," he laughed as he typed back.

The conversation went on for another half an hour. It turned out they had a fair amount in common. They watched the same reality TV show, Big Brother, and they both wanted the same contestant to win: Nicky. They also both turned out to be 14, or at least she said she was. The session ended when she had to go down for dinner. Caught up in the conversation, Ryan realised he hadn't checked her hito's name. He hoped he'd be paired with her in future, and able to recognise her if she wasn't wearing the jungle-themed attire. Maybe he'd get to meet her in real life too. He was starting to understand the appeal of Hito.

10,200 buki earned. Position: 213,061. Increased 751,763 places.

That was the most buki he'd ever earned from one session. When he bullied Gabby, he'd earned 9,600 buki. Perhaps the trick to the game was to kiss the other hito? Hito itself was still a mystery. A mystery that he was going to get to the bottom of. Tino6000 had to be a prime suspect.

Chapter 11

Teamwork

Ryan's alarm had already rung six times before he got out of bed the next morning. Mum was furiously shouting up the ladder for him to come down for breakfast, screaming that he was going to be late for school.

He unsteadily stood up from bed and rubbed his bloodshot eyes. He had been playing Hito until the early hours. It turned out to be surprisingly easy to lose track of time as he experimented with more actions within the game, such as dancing and hugging other hitos.

Tino6000 still hadn't made an appearance, but he would be ready for when they turned up in the chatroom. And now, as a more experienced player, he was feeling more confident.

At school, an unknown man stood in front of the room of black blazers. His lanky body nearly the height of the blackboard. The kids at the front tipped their heads back so they could look up at his face. His slim frame seemed unsteady every time the fan gusted in his direction.

"Mr Moore is feeling ill today so I'll be your substitute. I'm Mr Callaghan."

Mr Moore was never ill. Ryan couldn't think of a time when he had missed a lesson. Perhaps licking all that chalk had finally caught up with his digestive system.

"So how was it seeing your cousins on Saturday?" Ryan whispered leaning towards Cali.

"Huh," Cali said looking blankly at him. Cali was looking different today. His hair was messier, and one of his blazer lapels was sticking out.

"You said your cousins were round. That's why you couldn't come to Lorraine's?" Ryan scrunched his face.

"Yes, sorry. It was good. They've been coming around a lot recently," Cali said, looking back at Mr Callaghan.

Halfway through the lesson, Mr Callaghan excused himself to go to the toilet. As soon as he stepped out, the classroom launched into chatter. Tina, who was sitting next to Max as usual, pushed her chair away and stood up. She hit a ruler on the edge of the table five times.

"Guys. Attention, guys," Tina said as she slung the ruler back down to the desk. People turned to look.

"As you all know," she continued, "It's my birthday this Thursday. You're all invited of course. Even if I don't speak to you."

Max was deliberately looking away from her whilst everyone else stared. He played with the bendy ruler on his desk, flipping it backwards and forwards. Up and down.

"It's at Annabel's nightclub. I know you're all wondering why I'm still having this party, but Gabby was so looking forward to it. This isn't just my party but it's for her too. She'll turn up eventually and everything will be fine."

Mr Callaghan returned and shouted at Tina to sit down, and the class continued, behaving better than they did when Mr Moore was here. Ryan found that substitute teachers had a way of sticking so vigorously to the rules, never daring to move away from a set lesson plan. Also, there was no chalk licking or belly rubbing to distract you.

"I'm going to put you into groups for your homework assignment," Mr Callaghan said. This was unusual, a substitute teacher who was invested in setting homework. He pointed along different banks of desks, as if he were an orchestra conductor and his long finger a baton.

"You four," he said pointing at Ryan, Cali, Max and Tina, "You're a group." They all looked at one another before Mr Callaghan finished assigning the remaining students.

Five minutes remained of the lesson and Ryan stared at the clock counting the seconds.

"I can't believe she's still having the party," a whisper he heard to his right. He looked over and saw Amy speaking to her friend Jasmine. "It's so insensitive."

"Yeah, I would never have a party if you went missing," Jasmine said, "She was meant to be her best friend. And all that crap that it's for Gabby too."

"So tacky. We need to go, though. I'm sure there'll be some good gossip from it." Jasmine nodded in agreement.

The bell rang soon after and signalled the end of the lesson, everyone stood up and packed up their backpacks.

"Well, I guess we should figure out what we're doing, mates," Max said as he slipped his arms in his jacket, looking to his left at Ryan and Cali.

"Yeah," Cali said as the sun shone in on his copper hair, "How about we have lunch in the canteen and run through some ideas?"

"I can't imagine anything worse," Tina butted in, "Wasting my lunchbreak with you two."

Max tutted. "Lunch today then."

Ryan walked into the canteen. After looking around for a moment he saw Max and Cali sitting next to each other in the far corner, deep in conversation. He was a few feet away from their table when he saw Max nudge Cali's elbow. Cali stopped talking and turned to look at him.

"Oh, hey," Cali said looking red in the face, "How was Geography?"

"It was okay," Ryan said, pulling the seat out opposite them. "What were you chatting about?"

"Oh, just some ideas for this homework," Cali said. "Look, there's Tina."

They all turned around to see her appear at the double doors. She pouted as she pushed her way through a crowd in the middle of the room and stomped to the table. The chair screamed as she pulled it across the floor, from the table next to them.

"Let's get this done quickly," she said as she slammed her bag to the floor, "today isn't the day to do this."

The three of them looked at one another, not wanting to say anything to aggravate Tina further.

"Okay," Max said breaking the silence, "So we're supposed to discuss the main themes in *Of Mice and Men*. And then we each present one to the class. Anyone got any ideas?" he said, looking around at all of them.

"No!" snapped Tina.

"Well," Ryan said in an uncertain manner, "I guess dreams are a big theme. Lennie and George dream about being free, in a different life..."

"That's a good one, mate," Max said, "Do you want to do that? What theme do you want to do, Cali?"

"I guess another theme could be love."

"Go on, explain," Max said, flicking his blonde hair out of his eyes.

"The whole book revolves around the companionship between Lennie and George. It's paternal love, and George always has Lennie's back, even when he kills the puppy."

"Yeah!" Max said, "You do love, Cali. I'll do loneliness. Lennie and George. Candy. Curly's wife. I think everyone just wants to have someone."

"Yeah," Cali said to Max as he turned in his seat to face him. "We can put my section first and then yours because they fit so well together."

"I'm bored of this," Tina said, "What's my theme?"

Max smiled. "If we tell you, it kinda defeats the point of the assignment. You better think of a theme, otherwise we'll fail." Max snapped the book closed in front of them.

"Death," Tina said.

"Huh," Cali responded.

"Death. It's literally all through the book. The rabbit. The dog. Lennie. I listen more in class than you all give me credit for. You all think I'm thick."

Max nodded.

"*So* terrible that I have to present this theme with everything that's happening. How *will* I be able to hold myself together? Poor Gabby." Her tone bounced between sincerity and sarcasm.

"More important business," she continued, "You're all coming to my party on Thursday, right?"

"Erm…" Ryan said stuffing his hands into his trouser pockets, "I thought you wouldn't want me there seeing as we don't really know each other."

"Did you not hear me? Everyone is invited, and if Cali is coming you may as well come too. What's one more loser."

Wow. Tina might be a bitch, but getting invited to a party was cool.

"And you're obviously a geek," Tina said. "Don't worry, though, you can play Hito with the other geeks at the party."

He glanced over at Cali who rolled his eyes.

"Don't you play Hito?" Ryan said. He wondered again if she might be the infamous Tino6000.

"Yeah, I did a bit. Gabby was more into it than me. She's actually into a lot of geeky stuff if you get to know her." Tina sniffed. Ryan thought back to the diary entries and the argument that they had around Gabby not coming to Tina's birthday because of the charity night. He thought about what else they must have argued about over the years, and whether there could be anything else that would give her a motive. Was she honest in her police interview about the arguments that they had? She could have excluded it all and played the bratty best friend part. The party would be a good chance to get any more inside gossip, either from Tina directly or from some of her friends.

"Twenty minutes left of lunch," Cali said standing up, "me and Ryan need to go but good brainstorming session." He fiddled making his hair even messier before tucking his chair neatly under the table.

"Good? This brainstorming session has been gay," Tina mocked in her sarcastic tone.

"You shouldn't say that. It's rude," Max said.

Cali led Ryan away from the table.

"What? Where are we going?" Ryan asked as Cali led them out of the canteen.

"To the IT lab." Cali ran a few paces ahead of him up the stairs. They were deserted at lunchtime. Cali looked through the glass pane in the door of the IT lab and carefully pushed it open.

"We'll get in trouble if we're caught here on our own," Ryan said, cautiously pulling out a seat next to Cali at the computers. Ryan watched as Cali pulled up the browser and typed in Hito.

"Website blocked by administrator," the message on the screen read.

"You won't be able to get past the school's security settings," Ryan said.

"Oh, I will. I'll just go via a proxy which will trick the system." Cali was good with computers and sometimes pointed out the teacher's mistakes in IT lessons.

"I found something weird on Hito," he said, "I was on it last night in the chatroom. You always get someone who says 'pay'. I never understood why."

"Oh yeah, I've seen that too," Ryan said shuffling in his chair and pulling himself closer to the screen.

"Well, look what happens when you type it into the chatroom." A phone number popped up onto the screen. He mouthed the number. "How weird. I didn't want to ring it until we were both together. It could give us some more information about the game."

"We need to ring it." Ryan scrambled in his pocket for his phone, "I hope I have enough credit." He hurriedly pressed the numbers into the keypad. He held it close to his ear, with the ringing buzzing through him. *Ring ring. Ring ring. Ring ring.*

"Alright." A deep voice echoed down the line as Ryan jerked the phone from his ear and stabbed the speakerphone button, "What do you want?"

Ryan looked around the room as if he might get inspiration from something. "Erm..." he said. Cali moved his hands like he was playing Charades.

"Come on, lad," the voice continued, "I haven't got all day." The irritation in his voice was palpable. This didn't sound like someone who worked at a game company targeted at children.

"I typed 'pay' into Hito and this number came up," Ryan's voice trembled as both of them looked down at the call on the phone screen.

"Do you want to buy some buki? How much do you want?"

Ryan shrugged as Cali held up 5 fingers.

"Five hundred thousand buki?" Ryan nervously said.

The man muttered something inaudible, then came the sound of tapping at a keyboard. Ryan shared a puzzled look with Cali. "That will be £270. Do you have your parents' credit card so I can take the payment?" Ryan recoiled at the figure as Cali frantically stood up from his chair and snapped the phone shut. The call ended.

"We couldn't pay for that. It's weird, getting kids to use credit cards to pay for buki."

"Something isn't right with this game...," Ryan said as he tucked his phone back into his pocket and headed for their next class.

Chapter 12

Dinner

He stared at the toast. No matter how often he told his mum that he didn't like much butter, she would always lather it on like her nightly moisturiser. Pools of half melted butter sat on the anaemic toast.

"Why do you always do this," he snapped, holding up the plate.

"Ryan!" Dad said, "Don't talk to your mother like that. You can make your own toast in the future. You're fourteen after all."

"Sorry, son," she said in her usual loving tone. He couldn't help but smile at her. They were both going through a lot. Now wasn't the time to argue about toast.

"Anyway," Dad interrupted, "Whilst you're here we need you to be in tonight. Lorraine is coming around and we want to get used to being all together."

Ryan stared his dad in the face. What he wanted to say was, "I don't want to see your mistress," or "You can stuff it. I'm not coming to that dinner."

"Your mum will whip us up something nice," Dad said, putting down the crust from his toast. "Lorraine wants to get to know you better. And it'll help take her mind away from you know what."

"Fine."

"And none of your funny business. Asking her what she was doing that night. She wants her child back home. Tonight should take her mind off it. No questioning."

Ryan nodded but started to think of ways he could ask questions without Lorraine or his dad realising what he was doing.

School that day was uneventful, though Mr Moore was still off which was strange. Back home that afternoon, Ryan slumped in his computer chair keeping watch on the Hito chatroom. Tino6000 would be connected with him should they join the room.

"Ryan, she'll be here soon, come down," Mum shouted from downstairs. Ryan switched off the screen, dragged his feet down the metal ladder and took a seat on the sofa, still in his school uniform. Waiting for Tino6000 had distracted him from getting changed.

Dad came into the room and looked Ryan up and down.

"Nice to see you've made an effort."

Dad switched on the CD player in the corner of the room and gently slotted in a Frank Sinatra Greatest Hits CD. He started shimmying around the living room. His feet moving with the beat. Ryan pushed a cushion up to his face and let out a muffled scream. Dad grabbed the cushion and threw it onto the chair.

"Don't be such a spoilsport. You would have joined me when you were a kid."

"Well, I'm not a kid now," Ryan said.

Mum walked into the room and sat down next to Ryan.

"Remember they played this one on our first date? You were tapping your toes under the table." A small smile lit up on her face.

"When you find a girl, son, make sure she's amazing like your mother. She lit up every room she walked into. All the guys stared. A smile like Audrey Hepburn, eyes like Grace Kelly. You could have done much better than me, Donna. Much better."

"Well, I wasn't good enough, clearly" she said.

He grabbed her hand and went to kiss it, but she pulled away. The oven timer dinged, and she ran to the kitchen to check on the casserole.

The doorbell rang, and Dad hurried out as well. He heard Dad and Lorraine kissing in the hallway, and he grabbed the cushion back to cover his face. He heard him call her Mum's nickname; "baby." Ryan hoped more than anything, that when he did find his future wife, he wouldn't batter her self-esteem, waste the best years of her life and then ditch her for someone else. Kissing her in their marital home.

Dad and Lorraine came into the living room. She was wearing a T-shirt with nautical-style stripes and high-waisted jeans, plus a pair of stilettos. She looked like she was pretending to be French. Very out of place in Thurlcaster.

"Frank Sinatra!" she exclaimed. "Aren't you the best for putting our favourite artist on. You know, Ryan, your dad played this on our first date."

Ryan rolled his eyes.

"And what would the little lady like to drink?" Dad said, "Maybe something in a shot glass to start."

Ryan sat on the sofa uncomfortably fumbling with the stack of magazines next to him.

Mum called them in for dinner. The photo of Ryan's grandmother stared down at them from the wall, and the digital clock ticked off the seconds spent in hell.

"I know tonight isn't about this, Lorraine," Mum said, "But how have you been since Gabby's disappearance?"

"Yeah...it has been really...really tough. The house just feels so... empty. The police are just awful how they go through all of her things as well. She'll be so confused when she comes back, and everything is in a different place. I don't know what I would have done without Matt."

"Well, I'm pleased he's been good to you," Mum said.

"It seemed like you and Gabby were really close, Lorraine," Ryan said, realising this was his chance to crowbar information out of her.

"Oh, we are. We tell each other everything. She told me everything about her boyfriend Max. He checks in on me a lot which is nice. It's hard for him too. Her best friend Tina though. She's a complete waste of space. Don't even get me started. Best friend...my arse. Anyway, enough. How are you feeling about everything Donna? I'm sorry to intrude in your house. I know it must be a little awkward."

Mum looked straight at her. "Awkward? Absolutely not. We've all got our own stuff happening. I'm looking for a full-time job. And then I'm going to think about dating. Gosh I bet it's all changed now." Mum sat a little higher in her seat.

"Did you hear about the party?" Lorraine looked around the table. "Tina is... is..." she paused and shook her head before bursting out, "is still having her birthday party tomorrow! How disrespectful. You couldn't make it up, honestly."

Ryan looked down at his plate, prodding at the beef casserole with his fork. It would sound bad to say he not only knew about the party but was planning on going. He couldn't tell everyone that he was investigating Gabby's disappearance. How would he explain what had happened on Hito? His parents would never look at him again.

But Dad spotted his discomfort.

"Don't tell me you're going?"

Ryan continued to stare silently down at the plate.

"Answer me." Dad slammed his fist onto the table.

"Well…"

"Well, what?"

Ryan looked up to see all three adults were glaring at him.

"Everyone's going. I can't not go. I never get invited to anything. Gabby will turn up soon. Even Tina thinks she will." He locked eyes with his mother.

"I get it son, you want to go and have a good time-"

"You selfish boy! Lorraine is going through hell and you're off to a party!"

Ryan looked over at his dad. "I didn't know Gabby and it's not my party." He shrugged his shoulders as he gazed back down at his plate.

"You are a despicable little boy. It's time you grew up."

Ryan turned to his dad. He hated being patronised like this and his dad knew it. Ryan gripped his fork so tightly his knuckles went white.

"Selfish, selfish, selfish," Dad repeated.

"Matt please," Mum said. Lorraine sat uncomfortably looking at the clock.

"Shut up, MATT." Ryan threw down the fork. His dad jumped a little back in his seat.

"Don't lecture me. You're having an affair," Ryan said pointing to Lorraine, "and you play her the same song you played mum. Thinking Frank Sinatra was just for her."

"Stop right there-," Dad said, "this was meant to be a nice night for everyone."

Ryan couldn't contain himself. "You try to lecture me on decency. You don't care about me, and you obviously don't care about mum either. You were happy enough letting Gabby know about your affair, her probably telling the whole school, but you didn't have the balls to tell your own son."

Dad was breathing loudly through his nose, his fists still clenched and his face a deep red.

"Get upstairs. You're grounded." He jumped up from the table and pointed at the door.

"Come on Matt don't do this," Mum interjected.

Ryan jumped out of his seat, strode out of the room and slammed the door.

As he went up the stairs, he heard Lorraine call out to him, "It'll take some time to get used to all of this. Don't worry, we're all here for you."

He paused on the stairs. "Screw this. I don't want you here. I want things back to normal!" He stomped up the rest of the stairs.

Lying on his bed, Ryan's blood boiled as he thought about his dad. One thing was for sure, he definitely would be going to this party. If even only to spite Dad.

Chapter 13

Party

Ryan crept down the stairs the next evening, avoiding the squeaky fifth and eighth steps on the way. Dad was sitting in the living room watching darts on the TV.

Reaching the door, ever so gently he lifted the latch out of the ring. It was a real-life buzz-the-wire game. A single wrong move would set the buzzer off. He managed to get the latch out of the ring silently and then hung it perfectly next to the door. He then turned the key and opened the door...

"Are you going somewhere?" Dad shouted from the living room.

Ryan froze for a moment, then slammed the door behind him and sprinted down the street. His legs in overdrive. His dad wouldn't be able to keep up with him. After running for five minutes, he turned to make sure he was alone. It was clear.

He'd never been to Annabel's. Of course, it wasn't an actual nightclub; even a place in Thurlcaster wouldn't serve fourteen-year-olds alcohol. Annabel's was an under-18 club. The idea was you'd go there, get served soft drinks, dance and pretend that you were in an actual nightclub so you could feel like an 'adult'. Ryan didn't see the appeal.

He walked into the murky entrance, the old neon sign hanging above was missing the "b." It seemed like the whole school was here. He walked around the room, gently nudging people out of his way as he tried to find Cali. After ten minutes of looking, he finally saw Cali talking to Max at the bar.

After some small talk, which he really didn't enjoy, Ryan needed to pursue his investigations. Especially as he'd already risked so much coming here in the first place.

"So how you feeling about Gabby? Strange that she's still not showed up," Ryan asked.

Cali looked at him quizzingly. He knew Cali would be annoyed with him questioning Max; despite him not having a good reason to be so defensive of Max and sure of his innocence.

"I miss her. I just want her back."

"She was your girlfriend. That must feel so huge."

"Sure. Are you missing her, mate? Is that why you're asking?"

"Isn't it weird Tina's still having this party? When her best friend is missing?"

Max looked between Cali and Ryan. "Do we want to talk about this at a party? Or have a good time?"

"I'm just a bit weird I guess, sorry," Ryan said with a playful smile.

A group of twenty or so people were now in the middle of the dancefloor, hands waving in the air to the beat.

"I'm not brave enough to dance," Ryan admitted.

"Oh no, mate," Max said, "That's not bravery, that's just alcohol. You want some?" Max opened his check shirt jacket and lifted out a silver hipflask.

"No, thanks," Ryan replied hastily. He could smell the vodka.

He looked around and spotted a few hipflasks shimmering in people's hands. He had never drunk a drop of alcohol in his life, and this wasn't a good time to start. And the drunk dancers now looked stupid to him.

But drunk people might talk. Time to gather some intel.

Max spotted a friend and went over to him, leaving Ryan and Cali standing at the bar. Eventually the bartender took their order and handed them two Cokes.

More and more people kept arriving, despite the place already being packed. There was a mezzanine floor, and people were waiting on the steps to order a drink. The dancefloor with the electric blue strobe lights was rammed too, with everyone flailing around madly. The right-hand side of the room had brown sofas and tables. A long table stretched across the entire back wall filled with party food that still looked untouched. Ryan and Cali headed over to look at it.

A pink cake with four different levels stood towering in the centre, with each word of "Happy 14th Birthday Tina" piped onto it. This cake was enormous, but it still would not be enough to feed everybody here.

"Impressive, right?" a female voice said behind Ryan and Cali. They turned around to see a woman in her early 40s, with short black hair. The only person at the party holding a wine glass.

"We paid a professional," she said as she took a big gulp from the glass, a little spilling from the side of her mouth. She was drunk.

"I'm Tina's mum... Julie ...did I already say that? Who are you?"

They introduced themselves, Ryan feeling nervous around a drunk adult.

"How's Tina feeling about Gabby? They were best friends," Cali said jumping straight in.

"Friendships are hard...especially at your age.... god I would never go back." She gulped some more red wine. "You know Gabby wasn't going to come tonight? I mean if she didn't end up missing. That devastated Tina. Gabby always put herself first, and then everyone else second. That always got to my lovely Tina."

Ryan couldn't help but smirk.

"She was obsessed with boys, too," Julie said, taking yet another gulp from the glass. It was almost empty. "Tina liked Max. You know how much that hurt Tina? I bet that's why Gabby dated him. How can your best friend do that."

Julie tilted the glass and swallowed the last of the red wine. A droplet fell onto her white silk blouse, making it look like a splash of blood.

"Time for another drink!" She left them and made for the bar. She carefully took one step at a time in her enormous heels.

"Wow, I wasn't expecting that. Tina fancies Max. This could be the revenge I read about in the diary. Any idea where she is?"

They both scanned the room but could see no signs of Tina, aside from the photos plastered all over the walls.

"Do you think we'll find her?" Ryan said.

"She's bound to be here somewhere. She's too egotistical to not be at her own party."

"No, not Tina. Do you think we'll find Gabby?" Ryan's voice cracking with emotion.

"I hope we do. We need to keep investigating. The police seem pretty useless. If we don't find her, I doubt the police would think you did it because of those Hito messages."

"It's not even about that," Ryan said as he looked down at his Coke, "OK, so it was to start with. But reading those diary entries, and hearing more stuff about her... I just want her to be found and to be OK."

Cali patted his friend's shoulder.

Max was now on the dancefloor, and the rest of the football team had joined the chaos. The DJ announced that there was only five more minutes left to submit messages. He was collecting birthday messages for Tina that he would then read out over the microphone. Ryan recognised the DJ's voice; it was Vincent who worked at the local radio station, Thurl FM. His parents would religiously have his show on during Sunday mornings. None of these other kids would surely know who he was. Perhaps Julie chose him.

In the far left of the room, just away from the dancefloor, eight people were huddled around a desk. This was the first time Ryan had seen a laptop. The school IT lab only had desktop PCs.

They made their way over and saw the familiar blue loading screen of Hito. Circling around the desks, Ryan checked the name of the users in the bottom corner. None of them were called Tino6000. That would have been too easy. All the people at the desk started to raise their hands and say "in." They appeared in the chatroom at the same time.

As a few minutes passed, the game sent each person to their connection session. All but two were paired with others at the desk. The screens were filled with such varied scenes; a farm, a waterfall, a canyon. Partygoers stood watching over the screens to see the interactions of the hitos.

"I knew this wasn't a good idea," Tina said as she pushed through a few people on the outer ring of the watchers. Her black sequin dress sparkled under the strobe light. "Of course, you two would be over here," she said as she looked at Ryan and Cali.

She took a step forward and had to stop to catch her balance. Her eyes were glazed over. She sipped the sparkling liquid she clutched in her hand. They stood there silently watching, not knowing what to say.

"You haven't heard anyone say anything..." she paused, her eyes widening slightly as her lips stayed pursed closed, "say anything about Gabby. She can't ruin my birthday." She swilled the liquid around in the glass, a few drops flying out and hitting Ryan's shoe.

"No.... we haven't," Cali said.

"What would they say anyway?" Ryan asked innocently.

She stood there, still swilling her glass until a look of comprehension settled on her face. "Nothing. Gotta go."

She quickly pushed through the crowds of people watching the gameplay and headed up the stairs. She tripped on the second stair and spilled the rest of her drink. A spotlight caught her whilst she was halfway up the stairs as she was still steadying herself, the sequins on her dress glittering. The music fell silent. Everyone turned to look at Tina.

"Time for the birthday messages," DJ Vincent boomed out over the microphone, and applause rippled around the room. Julie carefully descended the stairs to meet her daughter under the spotlight. The DJ placed the submissions box on the front of the DJ booth for everyone to see. He shook it violently and then lifted the lid.

"First one...Happy Birthday, Tina. You're incredible and this party is amazing! Love Jasmine," he read out in his deep radio voice.

"Next...Happy Birthday, Tina. I hope in this next year you'll start telling the truth. I know what you're capable of."

Puzzled faces in the crowd turned to each other.

Chapter 14

Card

Chatter burst around the room. "What does that mean?" "Did she do something to Gabby?"

The microphone screamed as Julie grabbed it. "Right, time for some more music!" she shouted and then she handed back the mic and pushed the birthday messages box into the DJ booth where it fell to the floor. The DJ fiddled with a few buttons and then the Sugababes played through the speakers. The dancers resumed flailing their arms.

"Let's get our hands on that box. There might be something more inside," Cali said. He led the way over to the DJ booth and they stood chatting to each other, trying to act as casual as possible. After fifteen minutes, DJ Vincent opened the half-door to the booth and headed for the toilets. Ryan and Cali scuttled in, keeping their heads low, though everyone else was busy with Hito and dancing.

The messages box sat upside down in the corner with a few of the papers now spilled across the floor. The nasty message sat there face up. It was unsigned.

Ryan shuffled through a few more cards.

"Happy Birthday Tina"

"We know you did it Tina."

"Love that you have Hito here!"

"Max where have you hidden Gabby?"

"Max the kidnapper."

"Is Tina's mum drunk?"

The last card he looked at had no words on it, just a poor drawing of a penis. Ryan threw it to the floor, and Cali grinned.

"Wow, a lot of people think Tina did it. Or Max," Cali said rolling his eyes.

"Why are you so sure he didn't?"

Cali's face twisted, "I just don't think it's possible."

Ryan hurriedly picked up the papers scattered across the floor. "We haven't got time to read all of these. Let's take them and then we can look over tomorrow." He stuffed the cards into his trousers, his face wincing as he did. "We might be able to recognise some hand-writing when we have more time to analyse."

"There's one left," Cali dug a card out from the bottom of the box and handed it to Ryan. He grabbed the card from his hand and was about to stuff it into his pants, when he stopped. This one was different. It was in a sealed envelope, with "For Ryan Jones" wrote across it. It was for him. He ripped off the seal quickly.

'Ryan – I'll meet you in Mr Dhanial's office tomorrow morning at 8.30am.'

He felt lightheaded as he read the message.

"Did you put this in here?"

Cali shook his head, "No. What does it say?" Ryan handed over the card. "Wow! That's weird. How did they know you'd see it?"

"Maybe they thought it would have been read out over the speaker system? Either way, I'm going to be there. Come on, we need to get out of here before Vincent is back."

He took the card from Cali, stuffing it into his trousers too, before lifting the latch on the booth door and quickly making their way out. They re-joined the crowds of people as if they had been there all along. Ryan walking cautiously to make sure none of the cards dropped down his legs and fell out onto the floor. The DJ appeared twenty seconds later. It could have been a close call.

Cali disappeared into the midst of the party, consumed by the crowds of people. Ryan stood next to the Hito hub and watched the gameplay. It was amazing how addictive the game could be from just an observer's point of view. He saw Hito sessions play out, and candid conversations take place right before his very eyes. The players who connected would shout across the table ideas to get more buki. "Punch me," "kiss me," "I'm going to call you a freak."

He was engrossed. It didn't matter that he was standing by himself. He was at home with the other watchers and the players. They were connecting and he was a part of it. Albeit a silent part of it.

The temperature in the room was rising as more people gathered. Some to watch the Hito action. Many more to lose their inhibitions on the dancefloor. It was a split crowd. Ryan wiped the droplets of sweat from his forehead as he headed over to the door.

He stepped outside and the cool evening air hit him, refreshing him. As if he'd just stepped into a plunge pool. He sat on the wall facing Annabel's nightclub. The music trickling out into the street. The disco lights shot out from the windows. Red. Green. Blue. The colours of the rainbow one-by-one illuminated.

A thud sprang behind him, and he turned. A group of young men in their twenties were standing there. Two of them helping up their friend who had fallen on the path. He was incoherently slurring as he was lifted from the path and craned into the air.

"Look who it is," Ryan turned around to see Tina standing there. "What are you doing out here loner?" Her mouth was moving more than it needed to as she slurred her words. She clung to a drink in her hand.

A different one to what he had seen earlier. He stared blankly at Tina.

She stumbled to sit on the wall next to him. "Sorry, I don't mean to be mean."

"It's okay," Ryan said looking down to the ground. He could feel her looking at him. Staring at his face. Their eyes would meet if he turned his head. He rubbed his hand as a cold breeze hit them.

"You know, I wish I was you." She was still gazing at him intently. Ryan smiled and turned around to look at her, confused.

"If I was you, I wouldn't have these problems. Look at tonight" she continued.

"What do you mean?"

"People at my own party hate me. You heard that message. People think I did it." She tutted as Ryan remained tight lipped.

Another group of drunk men appeared behind, with both turning around to look. He wasn't sure how people could get into this state of being drunk.

She tipped her head back and took a big gulp of her drink. "You know. I always thought something would happen with me and Max. I guess he just doesn't like me like that."

This felt alien. Tina was treating him like a confidante. He liked it. But he couldn't help but unwind his thoughts on the investigation. Tina and Max's argument in the toilet could have been linked to Tina's fondness for him.

"You said in class that you think Gabby is fine. Why do you think that?"

She stared into her drink and shrugged. "I don't know. When she's done this before, she's never done it for this long."

"Done this before?" He squinted his eyes as a spotlight shone through the window.

"She's ran away before. It was tough for her when her dad died. She was more like him. When it was just her and Lorraine, there were a lot of arguments. She'd disappear for a few days and then turn back up."

Tina sprawled out her arms, and carefully stood up, balancing in her heels. She tucked herself back into the party, leaving Ryan sitting outside alone. Lorraine had done a good job at dinner of making it seem like her and Gabby had the perfect mother-daughter relationship.

By the time he got home later that night, he was happy to see that neither of his parents were awake.

As he walked through the hallway however, a piece of paper sat on the side table. He opened it.

'I'm disappointed in you. I know this is hard for you, like it is for all of us. You need to respect rules and boundaries, like my dad taught me.'

He tutted. All he wanted right now, was to get to the bottom of this mystery. No matter what rules had to be broken.

Chapter 15

Office

It was an early start to make sure he was at school before everyone else turned up at 9am. Dad wasn't at the breakfast table that Friday morning. Mum didn't bring up anything about the night before; she didn't ask about the party nor mention any of her thoughts around what he'd said to Lorraine on the Wednesday night. He appreciated that.

She did however mention the job interview she was going for this morning. It was at a rival cleaning agency for a full-time position. She sat there elegantly in a black dress, practicing her answers to potential questions. He helped out and pretended to be the interviewer at points.

Ryan left for school that day smiling and hoping that his mum's interview goes well. He walked across the empty yard and headed over to the staff block in building zero, where he had his first interview with the police last week. The corridor had a stench of concentrated coffee that drifted out the staff room. Chatter flowed out into the corridor, and he heard the teachers talking about some of the pupils. It hadn't occurred to him that teachers have a life outside of the classroom, nor chat about pupils to other teachers. It was strange.

He reached the top of the corridor and knocked on the door that read Mr Dhanial's name.

He didn't hear anything, so he gently pushed the handle. To his surprise, the young pretty face of Miss Wong met him as he entered. She sat behind her desk typing at her computer.

"Yes," she said as she peered down through her glasses, "It's a bit early for students to be here. Can I help you?"

"Mr Dhanial wants to speak to me," he said, whilst pulling on his backpack straps nervously. He didn't know who was going to meet him here. But he knew he needed to be in his office by 8.30am. He edged closer to her desk and could smell her floral perfume radiating from her. Each step closer to the epicentre. She looked back at the computer and typed into the system.

"What's your name?"

"Ryan Jones." She had no reason to know his name. He never had any contact with Mr Dhanial before. He wasn't a prefect nor was he someone that was akin to getting into trouble. She stared at the computer screen, tapping away at a few more buttons.

"I don't have you booked in. But if he has asked to speak to you, you can go and wait in his office. He's out at the moment but should be back soon."

She pointed to the door to the left of her desk. He stepped closer to her, his nose filling with the floral perfume, before opening the door to Mr Dhanial's office. It was the most underwhelming room he could have imagined. The secrecy surrounding the headteacher's office had marked many conversations at the school.

Apparently, he has a rabbit in the office with him. He has CCTV cameras where he watches the classrooms. The office has its own private vending machine, just for Mr Dhanial to use.

Any of those would have sparked some interest. Unfortunately, all he was met with was a few filing cabinets against the back wall, a sagging plant in the corner and the unspectacular desk in the centre with a desktop computer placed atop.

He sat in the chair facing the desk and the back of the computer. A clock ticked irregularly, the rhythm not staying exact to every second. Mr Dhanial must be a very tidy person. There wasn't a single piece of paper on the desk. He tapped his foot waiting for him to come. Another two minutes passed and there was still no sign of Mr Dhanial arriving. He'd occasionally hear

Miss Wong outside tapping loudly on her computer, her fingernails hitting each button.

A quiet rhythm played within the room. Ryan looked in every direction. It wasn't coming from the incoherent clock. What was it? This was a new beat to the room. He inched his head closer to the computer and realised it was coming from the speakers. He got out of his chair and walked around the desk to look at the screen. The blue loading bar of Hito was on the screen. Was Mr Dhanial really a player of this game too? He turned the knob down of the speaker so Miss Wong couldn't hear.

The screen loaded and a saloon like one of those in a wild west film filled the screen. It was like something that could have come straight from a Clint Eastwood film. At any moment he expected a shooter to push his way through the swing doors, with his boots tapping with every step. He could just imagine the horse tied up to the wooden post outside, and the ladies dressed in their heavy dresses. He panned the camera around. There was a dartboard in front of the wooden bar with hundreds of ales in the background all perched on their place on the shelf. He could just about hear the wild west music that leaked from the speakers.

Mr Dhanial's hito loaded fully and he was wearing a reflective metallic jumpsuit. Quite an odd choice, especially for someone so serious. A bald head that gleamed nearly as much as the jumpsuit he was wearing. Ryan scrolled down to see Mr Dhanial's username. Tino6000, it read. It was him.

The door of the office threw open.

"What are you doing in here?" Mr Dhanial imposed into the room. A silver watch shining on his wrist and his face reddening as he saw Ryan behind the computer. He jumped out of his skin and fell back a few paces.

"Please, I didn't see anything on the screen. I promise," Ryan said.

"Get out of here," Mr Dhanial continued to shout. Ryan paced carefully past Mr Dhanial and out of the door.

"Don't let anyone in without an appointment, Miss Wong."

He raced down the corridor and out the staff block. The air hitting his face with each stride. Reaching the top of the corridor that led out to the yard, he hurled the door open before hearing an "ouch."

"Are you trying to kill me, mate?" Ryan spotted Max's platinum blonde hair behind the door. "You need to watch where you're going otherwise one of the prefects will tell you off. What's the hurry anyway?"

"Nothing, just in a rush," he said, before he sprinted across the yard, trying to get as far away from the office as he could.

The clock ticked to 9.15am, as Ryan sat in his thoughts in class. Cali was saying something, but he didn't hear. He was living in a vacuum. Over and over replaying the image he saw on Mr Dhanial's screen and the hito. The silver watch that Mr Dhanial wore was the same as the metallic jumpsuit. Could this be a subtle nod to his character in the game?

A knock came at the door and Ryan still meandered in his thoughts. It wasn't until he heard his name being said that his consciousness kicked in. The same man as before appeared wearing the same hat. PC Gables. He called for Ryan, telling him to hurry up, as he tried to quickly make his way past the rest of the class. He followed him into the same corridor of the staff block where he had just been. He hung his head down to keep a low profile.

"You again. More trouble I see. This time with the police," Ryan looked up to see Mr Dhanial standing there. "What's your name?"

"Ryan Jones," he said, half looking up.

"Well Ryan Jones, I'm delighted to run into you again. I'm happy to tell you that you have detention on Monday for snooping. Keep your business to yourself." PC Gables scrunched his face as he listened. Mr Dhanial sailed off down the corridor with a stride to his step.

Ryan followed PC Gables into the small office that they'd been in for his first interview. DCI Binyon was already sat behind the desk, this time she wasn't in a uniform but a black blouse with her hair hanging down covering her ears. She was tapping her fingers on the table, her face focused. She didn't greet Ryan. He silently pulled out the chair opposite and sat down, with PC Gables taking a seat next to her. The seagulls squawked outside, and for a few moments those were the only sounds within the room.

"So, Ryan," she said still looking at the table, "Do you remember when we spoke to you last week?" Her tone was sharp, more direct than previously. Although now she was without uniform, she seemed more formal. She lifted her head and looked at him.

"Yes DCI Binyon. I do remember speaking to you last week." He pushed his glasses further up his nose, his hand shaking ever so slightly as he did.

She sighed.

"And were you completely honest with us last week about everything?" The sharp tone continued. PC Gables picked up his pen and hovered it above the notepad.

Ryan could feel his skin starting to itch.

Chapter 16

Blue Lights

"Yes...I was." He spat out those words as believably as he could. Lying was never a strength of his, but it had to be right now. PC Gables wrote something onto the notepad. Ryan leaned his head forward but couldn't make it out. The writing swirled like sea waves.

"Do you know what DCI stands for Ryan?" PC Gables said. The temperature of the room was rising, and with each tick of the clock, he was stepping closer to his doom.

"A Detective?" he muttered under his breath, trying to work out which path this was going to take.

"Yes, a Detective Chief Inspector, to be exact," PC Gables said, "Our job is to unearth any clues that may help a case, and also to unearth any lies any interested persons may tell."

DCI Binyon turned to her colleague. "PC Gables, I'm the detective here. Can you please focus on taking notes?"

"Well, I deserved to get the detective promotion," he muttered under his breath.

"Not right now Gables. Try to stay professional." She sighed.

This was a welcome distraction for Ryan. He tried to replay the conversation he'd had with them before in his head. PC Gables returned to hovering the pen over the notepad, waiting.

"Last time me and Gables spoke to you I asked you if you had played a game called Hito. You told us that you didn't. We're two weeks into Gabby's disappearance and the investigation has gone up another level. We've obtained a warrant for the game makers to tell us who registered the Ryan2005 Hito account, the last account that Gabby spoke to before she left the house that night."

"Yes?" Ryan gulped, his palms sweating. He flicked his index finger on his thumb, his arm shaking as he did.

"We found out the email account that the Hito belongs to. It belongs to Ryan Jones. It belongs to you."

Ryan scratched his forehead, feeling the sweat from his clammy fingers. He knew he must have looked red to them as he slinked slightly in his chair. His foot hitting the leg of the desk and sending an untimely clank throughout the room.

"Ryan, why did you lie to us?" she said, "You said you didn't play Hito and you did. Not only that, but you were the last person to speak to Gabby."

His face was flushed with a bright shade of red, his palms sweating faster than he could wipe them down. He was caught. Exposed. Did they know what he said to Gabby too?

"You look guilty," PC Gables said.

"Be quiet! I know you think I can't do my job. But I can. And I don't need your help," Binyon exclaimed, her hands hitting the desk. "We're just trying to figure it all out Ryan. Just tell us the truth," she said as a small smile grew on her face.

His eyes gazing around the room trying to find inspiration and confidence from something else.

"I do play it okay. I only said I didn't because you would think I was a suspect when I'm not."

He wanted to tell the police everything, but he knew it would make himself look worse. If they weren't already thinking he was a suspect, they 100% would after hearing how he had Gabby's diary entries in his bedroom. He had a motive.

"Ryan," DCI Binyon stared at him, "What did you say to Gabby that evening on Hito?" She pushed her hair that hung down onto her face and tucked it behind her ears. He could feel her body heat. PC Gables was still scribbling down some notes onto the paper.

"Just general chat. She didn't know it was Ryan Jones. I pretended to be from somewhere else. I'm being honest."

He couldn't be honest. He knew the implications and what suspicions may arise if he told them the detail of the conversation; how he threatened her.

"The game creator hasn't given us any details of the conversation yet, but if we find that there's anything else, we'll have another conversation."

PC Gables leaned forwards. "And it will be a lot worse for you then."

"GABLES. BE QUIET! Last time, please." She let out a gasp and sank into her chair. "One final question Ryan - why did you stop playing the game?" She tapped her fingers on the edge of the table again.

Ryan scrambled his legs closer to his body and folded his arms, asking her what she meant.

"Hito told us that the Ryan2005 account hasn't been active since the night Gabby went missing. Why have you stopped playing?"

"Erm . . . erm . . ." mist lay where his braincells should have. He couldn't pull a thought together. "Erm...I don't like the game. I hardly played it and don't care to play it again." He scratched his face and hoped it sounded convincing enough.

"Hmm...is there anything else you want to tell us?"

Ryan looked at both of their faces and then looked down to the hovering pen. "There is," he said. DCI Binyon leaned closer.

"I have a feeling I know who has Gabby, but I want it to stay anonymous." This piece of information he couldn't keep to himself.

"Go on..." she said.

"Your list of accounts of people that Gabby spoke to on Hito – I'm sure you'll see a Tino6000 in there. I was in Mr Dhanial's office this morning, and I saw the account loaded on his screen. That's why, PC Gables, you would have heard Mr Dhanial give me a detention for snooping."

"How do you know this account could be the person involved in Gabby's disappearance," she asked.

He couldn't say he knew because of the diary entries. And it wouldn't be believable to now change his story and say that Gabby told him directly – not when they knew he didn't know her very well.

"Please," he threw his arms to his side, "just look into Mr Dhanial. I think it could be him. There's nothing else I can add."

DCI Binyon stood up. "Thanks for your time today, Ryan." She gestured her hand towards the door, and Ryan took this as his queue to leave as fast as he could. He didn't think to say goodbye.

Chapter 17

Address

That evening Cali knocked at the Jones residence.

Mum answered the door, and he scurried up the metal ladder leading to Ryan's bedroom. Police presence had dominated the halls of the school, and Ryan didn't feel comfortable saying anything to Cali there. Films had shown him that it wasn't that hard to place listening devices under tables, inside walls, anywhere that could pick up a potentially incriminating piece of evidence that the police could use against him.

As soon as Cali's copper hair appeared at the attic hatch, Ryan couldn't help but explode.

"It's Mr Dhanial. It's all Mr Dhanial. I went to his office and Tino6000 is him."

"Woah, really!? Do we know how he did it? Or why?"

Ryan tilted his head. "Why else would a man of his age be on Hito? And remember how that girl on the

game told me that a teacher was rumoured to be playing it. It has to be him."

"What's our next step?" Cali asked, brushing his
curly hair away from his eyes. "Just leave it to the
police?"

"We need to find the makers of Hito," Ryan said as
if he'd been planning this in his head all day. "They
confirmed my identity to the police, they could tell
us Tino6000's. Then we can be sure whether it's Mr
Dhanial or not. Also, the makers could hand over to
the police the details of the conversation I had with
Gabby. I need to speak to them and stop them."

Ryan pressed the power button of the computer,
and the loud fan began circling.

Cali fumbled his phone out of his pocket, covered
the screen with his hand, and then hurriedly put it
back into his trouser pocket. He was acting weird.

The computer screen shook into life as the Windows opening theme blared out. They went to the Hito
website, but this time instead of loading up the game,
they clicked the "contact us" button at the bottom of
the homepage. It was so small that if you weren't looking for it, you'd never see it. Once the page loaded, a
miserable submission form filled the screen that would
apparently be answered within 7-10 days. There was
no phone number or email address. Not even a registered address. Was this why Hito had worked so slowly
with the police?

"What are you looking at?" Ryan said, as Cali opened up his phone yet again, before putting it back into his pocket in a hurry. Annoyed that Cali was distracted during such a key moment.

"Oh nothing," he said, "I've got to do something later, but I still have a little time." Cali was never so vague to Ryan. They tell each other everything, even if it was small and menial. What was going on?

Ryan googled Hito to see if there were any potential results for how to contact the game creators. A flurry of news articles trickled down the screen:

"The Mysterious New Game Taking Over Youngsters Lives."

"Why You Should Be Worried About This Game."

"Parents in Debt after Children Buy Hito Currency."

One article from The Independent caught Ryan's eye, "Are Adults Masquerading as Children on Online Game." He clicked through and scanned the piece, reading aloud to Cali.

"Perfect environment for adults to pretend to be children . . . children as young as eight have been known to play the game . . . no regulation of the contents of the game...suspicious 'buki' system generating millions but catching out parents...missing child in Thurlcaster."

Cali took this opportunity to check his phone again.

The last image on the article was a photo of Gabby stating how she'd been missing since the 13th of May.

"This game is a nightmare. It needs to be stopped. More and more is pointing towards Mr Dhanial. We just need to speak to Hito directly," Ryan said.

"I've got an idea." Cali jumped into life. He nudged Ryan's chair away, and then he took control of the keyboard. He went to a domain searching database and typed in Hito. An address popped up. Ryan edged himself closer to the screen as Cali tutted.

"It's not a real address. Hito bought this site from Buy-It domainz. This is their address listed, not the actual address of Hito," Cali said.

Ryan sighed as he slumped further back.

"Let me try one more thing."

Cali typed a few buttons into the web browser and then a grey box popped up to the side of the screen. "What we can do is determine the server location of Hito, which will most likely be the office address."

He typed into the URL bar and the grey box had different coding appear.

"A-ha." He highlighted a line of text within the code as Ryan leaned towards the screen. "That can't be it. It's coming up as Sheffield. Isn't this game from Japan?"

"What!? That can't be right."

They both stared at the address listed as the server location:

32 Dyme Street, Sheffield.

Ryan grabbed a notepad from the corner of the desk and scribbled it down, in a much more legible style than PC Gables'. Cali searched for any phone number registered to the address. Nothing. There were no businesses registered here. After ten more minutes of trying different wording into the search engine, nothing else appeared for 32 Dyme Street.

"It may be the UK server address. Or there may not be anything there. But it's worth a shot and there's nothing else to try," Cali said.

Ryan collapsed onto his bed. Cali pulled up a bean-bag and sat next to him. He couldn't resist looking again at his phone, with Ryan hearing the snap of the phone closing.

"I'm going to have to go now," Cali said, "we can go and visit Sheffield in the week. It's only a couple of hours away. I know it must be hard for you with everything going on. Especially with your dad dating Gabby's mum...."

Cali stood up from the beanbag and headed towards the metal ladder leading down to the main house.

"Cali?" Ryan said as he jumped off the bed, "How do you know my dad is seeing Lorraine?"

"Errr," Cali said with a crimson haze across his face, "I'm sure you told me."

"I didn't. I deliberately didn't tell anybody. Not even you," Ryan said, his eyes narrowing.

"You did. Maybe you're forgetting with everything that's happening." He shuffled around his hands be-fore saying goodbye and hurrying down the ladder.

The front door slamming on his way out sent a recoil through to the attic. Ryan knew he didn't tell anyone about his dad and Lorraine. Where was he going and why was he checking his phone all the time?

He needed to find out. He slipped his shoes on and ran down the metal ladder. He was going to follow Cali. Something wasn't adding up.

Chapter 18

The Chase

He raced down the stairs on his tip toes, and opened the door as quietly as he could. He didn't want to risk being caught breaking his grounding again.

Outside was dark now but he could see Cali turning at the top of the street. The streetlights buzzed beneath him. Ryan ran, his eyes occasionally looking into the illuminated living rooms on the right. One house had a picture-perfect family of four gathered around the table eating dinner. Their conversation flowing; they didn't notice him dash past.

He reached the top of the street and made the same turn. He saw Cali's head bobbing midway down the street. Reaching a back alley, Cali turned around and Ryan dived behind a car. He peeked his head up above the car and Cali was gone. The only way he could have gone was down the back alley. He knew that this only led to a residents' car park. Why was he going here rather than heading home?

Ryan edged down the alley. With each step he drew closer into the beam from the fluorescent floodlight that lit up the car park.

He was about to take another step when he saw a beer can in his path. Phew. If he'd stood on it, it would have alerted Cali that he was there. He pinned himself to the left-hand wall, trying to avoid the creeping beam. He could only make out a few cars in their spaces.

Slowly, he stepped away from the wall and emerged into the car park. The beam of the spotlight putting a marker on his head.

Cali wasn't there. Nobody was there. Cars sat in every space, but Cali was nowhere to be seen. Maybe he had gone a different way and not down this back alley at all. Ryan peered around, trying to see if any of the cars had their lights on. It was hard to make out from the heavy spotlight above, but he couldn't see any. He slowly stepped into the middle of the car park and did a full 360 degree turn but still there were no signs of life. Apart from the back alley that he came down, the only other way out would be to jump over one of the high back garden walls.

Exasperated that he had got this wrong, he turned and took a few steps towards the exit. He heard something. He stopped. It sounded like something scraping the ground. Maybe it was a bird or a cat. It was coming from behind the clothes donation bin in the corner.

He spun around and slowly approached, reminding himself that this may not be Cali but a feral animal, or a stranger who would be startled by his presence. As he stepped closer, he could make out a puckering sound. Walking as close as he could to the front of the bin, he still couldn't see what was happening behind. One tiny step at a time, he put one foot silently in front of the other, his shadow from the beam casting itself in front of him.

He could see Cali. He was kissing someone. His body was facing Ryan whilst the back of a blonde-haired woman faced away. He was shocked. They were so consumed in each other that they didn't hear that Ryan had approached him, nor that his shadow now loomed over them.

He stared, waiting for Cali to look up and see him. Cali cradled her body whilst they continued to kiss, each time getting more and more passionate.

"Cali?" Ryan said in a nervous manner, feeling like an intruder. Cali jumped as he removed his face from the blonde-haired woman, throwing his arms away from her.

"No, no, it's not what you think," he said whilst his voice croaked.

Cali's face twisted and emotion rippled throughout. Tears gathered in the corners of his eyes. He'd never seen him this upset before. The blonde-haired woman turned her head and Ryan got a look at her face for the first time. The blonde locks belonged to Max. Ryan stood there, his mouth ajar from the rest of his face. He was speechless. Max flicked his fringe away from his face with an equal level of vulnerability, his hand shaking as he did.

"Please, mate. We were just trying something out, it's nothing serious."

"It didn't look like you were just trying something out..."

"You can't say anything. It'll ruin us both. Please," Max said.

They both stood up and wiped the dirt that had gathered on them.

Ryan felt everything all at once. Awkward that he had interrupted such a private moment. Anger that his best friend had lied to him. A different person now stood in front of him. His hair colour looked different under this light too.

"Why didn't you tell me?" Deep sincerity rang through Ryan's voice. Cali fidgeted with his hands, first twiddling his thumbs and then putting them in his pockets. He looked down, avoiding eye contact with Ryan. His cheeks the brightest shade of red.

"It was just too hard to say. And you know, my African parents would kill me if they knew."

Ryan didn't know what to say. He went to speak, but the words didn't come out. Cali walked towards Ryan and spread open his arms to hug him. As Cali wrapped his arms around him, he pushed them off and stepped back. Cali looked at him with wide eyes.

It was too much to compute. He didn't care Cali was gay. But he had so many questions running through his mind.

"How long have you been seeing each other?"

Max and Cali each gave an answer.

"We aren't," Max said.

"A few months," Cali said.

They looked at each other, both with a puzzled look on their face. Cali frowned as he looked into Max's eyes. "We can be honest with him. I trust him."

Max firmly nodded before they turned their heads back to Ryan in unison.

"Don't tell anyone though, please mate," Max said, "It will destroy me at school. I won't be able to play on the football team anymore."

"I won't," Ryan said. "But all those times you cancelled on me to see your cousins; you were actually with Max right?"

Cali nodded ashamed, gazing at the ground.

"And this is why you didn't want us to look into Max as a suspect, even though he clearly had a motive to want Gabby to disappear."

The buzzing of the beam seemed to get louder. The smell from the bin washed over the scene, with rotten eggs and mouldy food taking over his nose.

"Look Ryan," Max interrupted, "I promise I have nothing to do with the case. Keep investigating. You're obviously onto some good leads. And, you need to clear your name."

"You told him everything! It was meant to be kept between the two of us." He breathed heavily through his nose as his whole body clenched.

"You have to un-"

"I get that you're gay, or bi, but you could have destroyed our case. I told you everything. And all of that time you were feeding it back to him. At any point he could have told the police and made it look like I was the one who abducted her." His voice croaked as his legs shook with adrenaline.

"I trust him. He would never try to frame you," Cali said as he grabbed Max's hand.

"But I don't trust him. Or even really know him for that matter. What if she found out he was gay and was going to expose him. There may be things he isn't telling you. You've only been with him for a few months. You could be his puppet. He could be behind everything."

Max blurted out, "I didn't do anything! I want Gabby to be found too mate. It's not easy for me. I was her boyfriend."

A light flickered on in one of the houses overlooking the car park.

"And what a good boyfriend you were. Maybe she would still be here if-."

Cali's mouth dropped open "Don't say that. You don't even know Max. He would never be capable of doing something to harm Gabby. It's not his fault."

Ryan took a step back.

"I'm now thinking it could be both of you. Working together. You handed me that card in the DJ booth, Cali. Did you plant that there and log into Mr Dhanial's computer to frame him for the job?"

"Ryan, you know that's not me," Cali said and took a step closer to him, "You've known me all your life. You're seeing suspects in everyone. This case is destroying you."

"No. I'm going at it alone now." Ryan took one last look at Cali, who's eyes were now ready to flow with tears, and then lifted his sticky feet from the floor and marched away.

Guilt riddled his body as he felt bad for being so sharp to them both. The guilt mixed with anger around being betrayed from the one person he had trusted. The sound of the flickering beam was accompanied by stomps as he made his way across the car park and back to the entrance of the back alley.

"Please," he heard Cali shout from the other side of the car park. Ryan's shadow reflected onto the path in front of him, and he realised that he would now be alone going forwards.

He worried cutting out them both like this would lead to them seeking revenge. But he had to take this risk, rather than the case being compromised further.

Chapter 19

Timothy Brown

He reached his house, and the gate weighed a tonne. His body lethargic, weak, like he'd been swimming at sea continuously for a week. He was overwhelmed. Incapable of thinking straight. He opened the door and it hit against the hallway wall. He threw his shoes next to the door and stomped up the stairs.

"You're meant to be grounded," Dad shouted from the living room, "Where have you been!? You've had your mum worried sick. Drop this rebel act. We want our old son back."

He heard Dad grumbling something else, but he was already onto the next floor and ready to climb up the metal ladder. It groaned as he threw one foot at a time onto each bar.

He did something he never did before. When he reached the attic, he pulled the ladder straight up to the hatch and then slid it into the loading contraption. A satisfying click was released. He lifted the dusty wooden hatch and snuggled it into the lips. He was now secluded.

He collapsed on the floor just next to the hatch. The shag carpet snuggled him. Everything had changed.

Beneath the fire in his eyes, he also felt a deep swelling of sympathy pulsating through his entire body. Cali was clearly going through a lot with his sexuality. He was sure this is not how he wanted him to find out. They never discussed girls or dating or anything like that. He understood that it would not have gone down well at school. He thought about the guy in year 11 that came out and was then followed home and shouted abuse at by a group of guys every night.

Ten minutes after lying there, he went over to the desk and looked at the notepad. 32 Dyme Street, Sheffield. He circled it with his black marker.

He loaded up the PC and the blue screen of Hito appeared, with the mysterious theme belting out the speakers like a church choir. He landed in the familiar chatroom as his hito Timothybrown. The blueish borders. The people messaging incoherent greetings. Some hitos running around for no reason. Twenty people or so were waiting in there. Waiting to be connected for their session. A few messages saying 'pay' popped up.

He scrolled the mouse over each of their hitos to see their names; James269, Darthkhan, Yourmum5. He scrolled his cursor over the second last hito. He gasped with astonishment. Tino6000, it read. The metallic jumpsuit from earlier today was now camouflage.

The clock ticked in the corner of the monitor. The connection session would start in twenty seconds. He remembered the trick Cali had taught him. Type CTRL + 7 and then enter their username. The loading bar popped up onto the screen, he pulled his chair closer in anticipation, hoping that he would be connected with this specific hito. He hadn't tried this out for himself. For all he knew, it could fail miserably, but he had nothing to lose and everything to gain.

The screen flashed black. Light flashed in bubbles on sections of the screen. His hito appeared in full form on the edge of a cliff. A galactic sized crater lay beyond the cliff, filling the view with murky shades of orange and brown. The sun was setting, hiding half of itself from the world.

He panned the view to see if there was any sign of digital life. In the rainforest he had to walk to the treehouse to find his partner, but there was nowhere to walk here. There was no building, no immediate obvious place to explore. He tried to walk inland but he couldn't get any further than a few metres before he hit an invisible wall. The view continued but the game didn't.

He panned the camera back to face the canyon with the setting sun. He wasn't sure if a hito could die, but he was going to find out. This might be his only opportunity to speak to Tino6000, or Mr Dhanial.

One step. Two steps. The world spinning as Timothybrown tumbled down the cliff. The orange and brown shades all merged into one bewildering shade of trauma. Exclamation points were auto typed into the speech bubble above his hito's head. He'd made a mistake. This definitely wasn't what he was meant to do.

The screen faded to black. Ryan sighed. He moved his cursor to the exit button. He'd wasted his one chance. Maybe if he'd been a little more patient and waited at the top of the cliffside.

The black screen was now fading to a brown. His hito was there, standing upright. He was at the bottom of the crater. He panned the camera once the scene fully staggered into place. Nothing but jagged rocks where the setting sun clashed with the impending darkness. A cave buried deep into the cliff face stood behind him. Impossible to see from the top. He approached the cave and headed inside, burying himself in its darkness. A small crack of light appeared. Walking towards the light, with each step glowing the screen a little more, candles appeared and lined the route. Before him now stood Tino6000.

"Did you request me as your connection partner?" the bubble read above his head.

His fingers slipped off the mouse. Was there a way for Tino to know this was him despite creating a new account? Had his disguise been unearthed?

"No" he typed back, "Why would I do that? I don't even know you."

Three bubbles appeared over Tino's head. They disappeared then reappeared.

"Sorry," the first bubble read, "force of habit. Your name's Tim, I guess. Mine is Bob."

Bob? He knew that Mr Dhanial's first name was Saj. Was he purposefully lying about his name? But why would he lie to a complete stranger? There were no Bobs at Castle Montgomery School. He couldn't even think of a Robert. Besides, if it wasn't Mr Dhanial, what kind of fourteen-year-old was called Bob. This was clearly a disguise. He needed to approach Tino in a non-suspicious way that could help garner more information.

"So, you live in Thurlcaster I guess?" he typed.

Within an instant the bubble appeared, "yes" it read. He knew he was on the right tracks.

"Did you hear about Gabby going missing?" Ryan typed, not sure if he was about to scare off one of his most likely suspects.

The bubble did the same dance again, appearing and disappearing. Whatever Bob wanted to say, he was thinking very carefully about it. Was he worried about incriminating himself?

"I did," Bob wrote, "I knew her quite well. In real life and on here."

Ryan's eyes widened. His fingers hovered over the keyboard. He performed the same dance as Bob. Typing, deleting, re-typing. He had to phrase this perfectly.

"Did you have to speak to the police too?"

"Yes."

His heart picked up rhythm once again. Adrenaline soaring through his body. This was his chance. He now knew they were also a person of interest to the police.

"Can you show me your face?" he typed, the cave seeming smaller than ever before as the candles flickered on the sides. All he needed was Bob to type back using the keywords "show" and "face," and that should be enough for the webcam to kick in silently.

He waited. The three dots appeared. Disappeared. The same dance...

"Why would I show you my face?" the mysterious stranger typed.

He had them. It was now time to unveil this man. Or woman. The outline of a grey box popped up above Tino6000's head and a sand timer appeared in the middle. He couldn't contain his anticipation. He stood up and pushed the chair away and gripped the edge of the desk.

The sand timer disappeared. No one filled the box. It was black. Why couldn't he see their face? A buzzing sound came through his speakers. He had an audio link. A vibration reverberated through the system. And then he heard the typing on the keyboard. He jumped as a loud noise came echoing through the speakers. It was a cough, so deep and loud that he couldn't imagine it ever belonging to a woman. They must have stuck something over their webcam to hide their image. He just had to wait for them to say something. He may recognise their voice.

"Do you want to be better at this game?" Bob wrote.

"Yes?" he typed back confused.

"I can get you some buki..."

Deep breathing filled the airwaves. In. Out. In. Out. He saw the three dots appear again above the hito. A rustling came through the speakers, and Ryan leaned in closer as he heard some very faint muttering. He couldn't make out what they were saying, and it wasn't loud enough to recognise. The rustling stopped. Tino6000 vanished in front of his eyes and the loading screen took Ryan back to the chatroom.

1,900 buki earned. Position: 161,002. Increased 23,059 places.

Glancing to the corner of his desk he saw the cards from Tina's party. On the top lay the card that led him to Mr Dhanial's office earlier that day. Grabbing it with both hands he stared at the curls of the handwriting. He spread all the other cards on the table. This handwriting didn't match any of the other cards. He knew he recognised the writing from somewhere. But he couldn't place it.

Chapter 20

Family Time

Ryan awoke early the next morning, largely due to the half a dozen birds that perched on his attic window and had been singing since the break of dawn. It was Saturday and no school meant that he could focus on what he needed to plan. How and when he could go to Sheffield.

He dragged himself out of bed and made his way to the computer. He pushed the cards aside and dropped his keyboard to the front of the desk. As the desktop loaded, an MSN window popped up. It was from Cali.

Cali: *I'm so sorry again. I didn't mean to break your trust. I promise I have nothing to do with this case. Let me know if there's anything I can help with. I won't tell Max whatever else we find out. I promise. Just me and you as always.*

He read the message and moved his cursor over each word as he did so. This was painful. If he could type and say everything was fine, he would. But he couldn't.

He closed the chat window. A yellow flashing still lit up the bottom of the screen. He clicked it and noticed there was another chat. He gasped when he read it was from Thurl123. They hadn't been heard from since that first threatening MSN message. His heart picked up pace.

Thurl123: *I know you know more than what you say. You're doing an investigation. Give it up now. Or else. You don't want the consequences, trust me. I'm keeping a close eye on you. A closer eye than you may think. Tip: the police won't look at you too kindly if they discover you have Gabby's diary.*

It must be someone close to him. He scribbled on the notepad. It could be Cali; he did have a motive. He wanted Max all to himself so it would have been convenient for Gabby to disappear.

Max had a lot to lose. He really didn't want the school to know about him being gay. He'd likely have to leave the football team.

Tina was still a big suspect. Max could have been passing on the investigation updates to her. She and Gabby clearly had a lot of issues in their friendship, and a lot of people thought that she had a part to play as he saw from the anonymous box.

He sat contemplating and then flipped over his notepad. It was impossible to pinpoint who Thurl123 was right now. He had to focus on how he could get to Sheffield. This was the next obvious step.

Before he could type into Google, Mum shouted up the stairs for him to come down. Reluctantly, he came down the cold metal stairs of the ladder and then slid around to appear at the top of the staircase.

"We're off to a car boot sale love. Get your shoes on."

"I'm not coming. They're hell," he said shaking his head.

"Well, hell it is then. Hurry up."

She grabbed her jacket and opened the front door. He forced his feet into shoes.

The car ride was silent all the way there. Ryan purposefully sat behind his dad so he couldn't see him as clearly, and he was sure Dad was happy with that too. Tension still lay in the air from the bubbling conflict with Lorraine and from breaking his grounding. Twice.

It took him a while to realise that they were heading nowhere near Archmans field where the car boot sale was usually held. Instead, they were going straight into the town centre. The car stopped in front of a Georgian style building as Dad pulled up the handbrake and took off his seatbelt.

"This isn't the car boot. Why are we here?"

Neither of his parents replied and instead both continued to get out of the car. With no other choice, he followed suit, looking around his surroundings quizzically. They walked up to the building in front of them and knocked on the door. There was no sign on the door. No signal as to what lay inside. It looked like a normal, well very nice, house.

A curtain flickered on the open balcony upstairs. He heard footsteps coming towards the door. It creaked open and a middle-aged man with silver grey hair stood before them. He was wearing a tweed suit and had the most manicured hands Ryan had ever seen. Each fingernail perfectly sized with white tips.

"Hi, you must be Donna," he said in a deep husky tone, "And I'm guessing this is Ryan and Matthew."

"It's Matt," Dad said.

The man's oud aftershave wormed from the house. Ryan tried to peer inside, trying to guess what they were all doing here.

"Come on in," he said as he gestured them inside. He stepped in and was met with dark wood panelling adorned on the hallway walls. A bear head stuck out of one of the frames, and a huge grandfather clock sat next to it. They went into a side room that was ordained with just as much eclecticism. Light flooded in through the bay window, and a chesterfield sofa dominated half the room, with a single brown leather chair facing it.

"If you all sit down on the sofa, I'll grab you a drink," he continued with his deep voice.

The man came back with four cups carefully entwined within his fingers. As effortlessly as he walked, he equally as gracefully handed each of them their respective drink. He stood in front of his chair, keeping his legs tight together, and descended onto it with class.

"I'm not sure how much your parents have told you, Ryan" he said whilst taking a sip from his own cup, "I'm Dr Midler. I'm a trained psychologist and I'm here to facilitate you all speaking effectively as a family. I hear you've had a bit of a tricky time recently."

Ryan turned his head to his parents, both deliberately ignoring his gaze and looking at the psychologist.

"There's a lot happening," he continued, "The new relationship that your father has with Lorraine. This seems to have signalled a change in you. They're worried for you."

Ryan shrunk into himself. He wanted a hole to appear beneath the sofa and swallow him up. He didn't want to talk about this. Did his parents really think having a family counselling session would solve everything?

"I don't want to do this. This isn't going to help."

He was so annoyed that they had brought him here.

"Come on, son" Dad raised his voice, "We need this. It's killing your mum that you've been behaving like this."

Dr Midler held his hand up to the three of them on the sofa, to what Ryan deduced must mean to not say anything.

"Here I have a stick," he said as his hand displayed a stick that you'd find in your back garden. "This isn't just any stick. It's the stick that controls who speaks within the room. When I give you the stick, you can speak."

A laugh nearly erupted from him. Ryan had only ever seen something like this in a film. He didn't think this was a technique they used in real life.

Dr Midler stood up as gracefully from his chair as he had sat down and approached the sofa. Readying himself for a fight, Ryan started to think what he'd say when he was given the stick.

Confusion circled over him when Dr Midler handed the stick to Mum. She held it in both her hands and then started to weep. Tears rolling down her face like a fountain, hitting the floorboards and sinking into the wood.

Dr Midler encouraged her to let it out and she did. Five minutes passed of her crying. The stick now covered in tears too. No words came out, just illegible muttering when she would try to speak, and then the crying would fully take back over.

Ryan wanted to comfort her, but each time he tried to speak, Dr Midler raised his hand for him to be quiet.

He hated seeing his mum like this. And knowing this was all his fault.

The crying finally cleared up and she looked directly at Dr Midler.

"I...I...I...I blame Matt."

Ryan's eyes widened and Dad sharply turned his head to stare at her.

"This relationship has ruined my life and ruined my family. God, I hate Lorraine for doing this to us. No wonder Ryan is behaving how he is."

Ryan's eyebrows arched. Frown lines appeared on Dad's face. Dr Midler being ever the professional decided that this was parent's business, so Ryan was swiftly sent from the room to allow them to have a private conversation.

He wasn't called back in. At times he heard the odd sentence being shouted, "you did this to us," "You've ruined us," and then silence would once again descend onto the hallway. This wasn't about him; it was about them.

After forty minutes, Mum and Dad swiftly made their way out the door. Mum marched five paces ahead, as Dad slung his head down.

Ryan had time to make his plan whilst they were having their session.

"I'm going to stay in town for a bit. I'll be back home later," he said.

They both nodded as they fumbled into the car wordlessly, consumed by their own troubles. He walked past the row of Georgian homes and headed into the centre of town. The worn-down buildings, grey with pebbledash front, slouched in the main square. Their expiry date far in the past.

Thurlcaster was not a place he wanted to spend his life. He had dreams of living somewhere brighter.

The scene of his mother crying at Dr Midler's would pop back into his head, and he'd try his best to block it out and distract himself.

Without thinking of the route, he headed for the bus station. Busses roared as they flew past. As he reached the national busses ticket office, a young man only a few years older than him, leaned down from the booth.

"Do you have any busses going to Sheffield?" he asked, eager to know when he could embark on his investigation.

The man clicked his mouse a few times and typed into the screen. He chewed gum loudly as he looked up the bus times.

"All of the busses are sold out. Seems like there's a mass exodus from Thurlcaster. Who can blame them though, ey? Next one isn't until Tuesday at 9am. £12 for a return."

Ryan scrambled in his pockets and then pulled out a collection of coins. He placed each one on the booth as he counted out loud. The young man sighed, whilst looking at the queue that had grown behind Ryan.

"£12 exactly," Ryan said as he pushed the coins towards him.

The man didn't even bother to count the coins and placed them into his cash register drawer. The printer cackled like an old motor car, and he grabbed the tickets.

Tuesday couldn't come around fast enough. He hoped when he got home, his parents would be in a better state too. For everyone's sake.

Chapter 21

Body

Pancake Sunday was cancelled the next morning. The missing pair of shoes in the hallway showed that Dad wasn't in the house. After a disappointing bowl of wheat, he flicked on the TV to see which Sunday morning cartoons he could watch.

His favourite show was called Grizzly Tales for Gruesome Kids. Given everything that was happening in his life, something more upbeat would be helpful. Before he could decide what to watch, the local news appeared on the channel.

"A body has been found at Robins Wood in the early hours of the morning. Speculation has arisen that this could be the body of missing student, Gabby McGee, who went missing on Friday 13th May, over 2 weeks ago now."

Ryan threw the remote to the side of the sofa. He could feel his chest muscles tightening. This was awful. He couldn't imagine the possibility that she may be dead. He ran up the stairs and climbed the metal ladder, his knee hitting a few of the bars on his way up.

Wading through the shag carpet, he mounted the desk chair. He searched in the PC for 'body found Thurlcaster' and was met with a range of similar results. Clicking from article to article to see if there was any more information to feed himself. They all said the same story. All accompanied with the same smiling photo of Gabby.

He got out Gabby's diary and lay on his bed. The three entries that were now crinkled pages. Ryan had lost count of the times he had read her words. He could probably recite them from memory.

I don't feel like I belong. I feel like my life is pretend and I just act a certain way to please others. This was the line he connected to the most. As he read it repeatedly, he started to cry. One of his tears hit the page and he wiped it away, trying to avoid any damage to the sacred text.

When his crying stopped, he looked through the rest of the entries. The passage around her not feeling close to Max was so much more pertinent since finding out that he was gay.

He closed the diary and felt a huge sense of loss. This would be the closest he would ever connect with

Gabby, through her inner thoughts rather than in-person.

For the rest of the day, he lay mostly still. His body sometimes shaking from the occasional cry he would let out. After an uncomfortable, and mostly restless, night's sleep, he walked through the pendulum of the school gates.

A sombre air washed over the yard, and he knew what to expect. Around 60 people were gathered into the classroom caravan. The caravan sat just off the school yard and housed classes temporarily if a room had maintenance, or any other issue. The room was cold. No decoration, just a single desk at the front and chairs stacked to the sides of the room. The students shuffled around. Every footstep circulated throughout the dense floor and into the wafer-thin walls.

Mr Dhanial strode into the room and all the students turned to face him. Ryan, and he's sure everyone else, worried whether this would be the confirmation of her death. Mr Dhanial stepped in front of the desk, his ageing features looking harsh.

"Some of you," he started before letting out a dry cough, "may have seen the news yesterday. We've decided to bring together those of you who were present in many of Gabby's lessons to update you on some news. A few people who were very close to Gabby have been told separately. The police have asked me to provide you with this update, but please remember that this is just for yourselves."

He looked down at the sheet of paper he grasped in his hands. The paper wobbled as his hand shook.

"A body was found in Robins Wood yesterday. Unfortunately, without going into too graphic of detail, it's very hard to identify who this could be. Visual identification has been attempted by close family, but this has been unsuccessful. They're hoping that DNA can be successfully tested but this may take some time."

Ryan closed his eyes as he heard those words. She could still be alive.

Whispers rippled around the room at Mr Dhanial's news as people covered their mouths. One girl in the corner was crying as a group of girls stood around her. Cali was standing a few rows behind, and Ryan could see he was trying to gain eye contact whenever he turned around. He looked away from him each time. He wasn't ready to forgive him for telling Max everything.

"If you don't feel up for being at school, please speak to me privately and we can discuss options. Also, remember that our on-site counsellor is available at any time to speak. We'll keep you updated."

The dust danced in the air as the students made their way out of the temporary room and back to classrooms. Tears were being wiped from cheeks as they headed to their lessons. This was all so strange.

Ryan reached the top of the stairs and saw that Mr Moore was now back in English Literature class.

"A nasty case of flu. So, what did this Mr Callaghan do with you all then?"

He picked up the piece of white chalk at the board and licked the side of it, the whole class grimacing in disgust. Ryan quickly wished that the substitute teacher was back. Mr Moore pulled down the roll-down blackboard and revealed the homework that had been set.

"In groups present back the main themes in Of *Mice and Men*. Well, I guess we'll do this then. I've had no time to prepare lesson plans. Get in your groups, whatever groups he assigned you in, hurry up."

Ryan was surprised to see that Tina and Max were in class. They dragged their seats to sit opposite Cali and Ryan. He didn't want to be here, though he was sure they didn't either. Cali had awkwardly sat next to him in silence for the lesson up to this point, and he wasn't in the mood to pretend that all was fine with him. He tried not to look at them both, the feeling of betrayal still pulsing throughout his body.

"10 minutes for each team to finalise your presentations," Mr Moore shouted before going back to typing at his computer.

Ryan shuffled in his chair when something hit his knee.

"Sorry," Max said under his breath, "that was me. Accident of course mate."

Ryan didn't reply, instead choosing to watch Mr Moore manically type on his keyboard. He was certain he would be looking at some new chalk to buy. The silence continued. The conversation from the other teams in the room made the silence more noticeable.

"Today is a bummer hey. I begged my mum to let me take today off. I knew they would drag me and Max to one side and pretend that they had all this support. Really, they have nothing."

None of them said anything. Ryan looked at her with deep set eyes.

"I feel like I'm missing something here. Something that isn't Gabby. Spill the goss," she said whilst taking a moment to glance at each of them. They all remained silent. "Come on, I could do with perking up."

Ryan decided to look down at his notebook and to memorise his theme; dreams. It couldn't be a more apt theme seeing as he dreamed of solving this investigation and dreamed of finding Gabby.

He hated presenting. It was usually his number one fear, and he would be petrified whenever he would be forced to present. Today though, the fear bobbed up before thoughts around Gabby would pop up higher in his head.

Mr Moore called Max and Cali to the front of the room, and they scurried as fast as they could; anything to get away from this silence. He edged over the front of his desk to see if he could hear what Mr Moore wanted.

"What is up with them? Something fishy is happening," Tina said.

Ryan shuffled in his seat awkwardly again.

"I don't know what you're talking about Tina. I think it must just be the shock from the news."

"It's not that. What I'm talking about is Max and Cali. They would never have been friends before and now look at them. They've got close since Gabby's disappearance. It's weird timing, right?"

Ryan sat looking at her, performing his best acting of "I don't know what you're talking about" face.

"I think they did it. I think they killed Gabby and now they have to be friends. They're scared the other person will tell someone if they don't stay close."

"What!? I don't think that's it. You can't just say that," Ryan said as he looked around to see if anyone had heard her.

"Well, you explain to me why suddenly they're friends. And it looks like you haven't said a word to Cali today. Is he distancing himself from you?"

"No, we're fine." He lied again.

"Max used to speak to me all the time. He'd message me all hours of the day. Not anymore. He might have a new girlfriend, that's why he had to get rid of Gabby.

What if Cali covered for him?" She flicked her brunette hair and tilted her head.

Max and Cali both approached the table and Tina dropped herself in her chair crossing her arms, staring at Ryan with her "I know I'm right about this face."

"Our group is going first," Max said.

Ryan nodded, his first sign of acknowledgement to him.

A knock came at the door, and everyone spun their heads around. In stepped the always smiling Miss Madison. Her beamingly white teeth flooded the entire class, her sweet eyes like a kind neighbour with her hair in angel curls. Her dress touching her ankles and her flat black shoes strapped safely to her feet.

"Sorry to disturb you all," she said looking at the class. "Bob, can I borrow your two-metre ruler please?"

Mr Moore didn't look up from the computer and lazily gestured his hand to where it was next to the blackboard. She grabbed it and scampered out, taking her glowing smile with her.

Tina and Max had begun talking about the project, but Ryan was too focused on what he had just heard at the front of the room. Bob. Mr Moore was called Bob. Could he be the Bob from Hito?

Before he could spiral further into his thoughts, his group were called to the front by Mr Moore. Or Bob as it turned out.

They all stood up in unison and dawdled to the front of the room, none of them looking particularly enthusiastic. Ryan stood there and looked out to the sea of bodies. Each one seemed to be staring back at him. Ready to judge what he would say. Laugh at him if he was to say something wrong. Was he sure that 'dreams' was a good theme to discuss *with Of Mice and Men*? The piece of paper in his hand rustled as he swayed it from side to side.

"So...so," he said with his voice croaking, his nervousness growing, "I guess, our first theme is dreams. And that is because-."

A loud knock interrupted him. Everyone turned to face the door. Was Miss Madison returning the ruler already?

He swivelled around as the door opened and saw the sharply dressed DCI Binyon standing there. Her eyes caught his and she smiled.

Chapter 22

The Station

"Ryan Jones. Can you come with me please?"

He gulped as his face crumpled. He took a step towards her, his legs feeling weak. She sounded more serious than she ever had before.

"You may want to bring your bag and jacket with you."

In panic he dropped the paper to the floor and went to grab his things. Looking out the window, he saw the blue lights twirling atop the police car. The jacket felt clunkier than ever. He carried the weight and looked over at Cali who was standing at the front. Shock was written all over Cali's face; his mouth open. When he noticed that Ryan was staring, a comforting smile appeared on his face. He was there for him, even though Ryan hadn't been there for him recently.

They left the room and the classroom door slammed behind them.

"What's this about?" Ryan asked DCI Binyon. His hands tugged at his backpack straps as he hurried alongside her.

"You'll find out once we get to the station," she said monosyllabically, not giving anything away. He fidgeted more with the backstraps as she marched him onto the school yard. A few rogue students mid-walk stopped in their tracks to gaze at him with the police officer. He wondered, as much as they must have, why he was heading to the police station.

The police car was parked conveniently in the middle of the yard, with the surrounding buildings overlooking it. He could see people within the classrooms gathered around the windows as he ducked and slid into the back. His backpack on his lap, as he wrangled his arms around it like a teddy bear.

The metal bars between him and DCI Binyon felt intrusive. Criminal. Although the sirens weren't on, the blue light spinning around on the top were reflecting into all the windows. He imagined he could hear the siren, sounding the alarm to everyone on the street. When it finally reached the station, he jumped out as quickly as he could.

DCI Binyon asked him to sit in the waiting room whilst she went through a door to the left of the reception. Gazing around the room he saw an eclectic mix of people.

A girl in her mid-twenties was sitting alone crying in the corner. She reminded him of his mother at the family counselling session. It was difficult to make out if she was the offender or the offended. A middle-aged man with greying hair sat on the other side of the room, twiddling his thumbs and flashing his wide eyes from side-to-side.

Ryan never thought of himself as much of a homely person, but right now all he wanted was to be sitting at dinner with his mum and dad. He wouldn't mind Lorraine being there too.

DCI Binyon came back into the reception, and without saying a word signalled for him to follow her. She went back through the door which led into a clinical corridor. When they reached Interview Room #6, she stopped. His palms were starting to collect sweat, rubbing against the plastic of the backstraps that he couldn't stop playing with.

The metal door swung open, hitting the brick wall on the other side. PC Gables was there. Ryan looked down at the desk and saw it. Sitting there in the middle, the swing light making it a brighter shade of pink; it was Gabby's diary.

He took his place at the table and looked at Gables and Binyon, rather than looking down at the guilty diary staring directly back at him. He tapped his fingers on the table.

"I just want to make it very clear, we at this point aren't interviewing you as a suspect, but as a person who may have valuable information. Do you understand that Ryan?"

He nodded back to her as he could feel his fingers turn to slime.

"We've brought you here today because there's a very important piece of evidence that has come to light. Something that we didn't want to bring to the school, and instead wanted to keep within the safety of the station."

The room was grey, but his thoughts were colourful. Ideas of every kind of question that they could throw at him were lit up around the room. Like a gameshow but one that the contestants would never volunteer to be on.

"Do you recognise this?" she said holding the pink diary up to the light.

PC Gables was in his usual position with his black fountain pen hovering over the notepad.

Ryan sat there, not knowing how best to answer the question. His mind not working fast enough to make up a lie. His fingers continued tapping, creating a rhythm for the interview. One minute passed very slowly.

"Let me give you some background to why we're asking this. Gabby is still missing, but we're examining a body that was found yesterday in Robins Wood. I'm sure you saw it on the news and heard Mr Dhanial brief the school about it today. This investigation may very quickly turn darker. A missing person case carries hope and positivity. Everyone who can help is spoken to. A murder case...well it's what it says."

He nodded.

"This book here," she said waving it in her hand again, "was found on your bed by Lorraine. We understand that her and your father are in a relationship. She was very confused as to why you would have it. We can confirm it's her diary because her name, in her handwriting, is written on the inside cover."

Of course – when he was reading it last night, he forgot to hide it again. How stupid. What was Lorraine doing in his room any way? A drop of ink leaked out of PC Gables' pen and onto the notepad, creating a puddle sized smudge on the crisp white paper. The rhythm of the room stopped and his hand lay rest on his lap. He couldn't concentrate with his hand tapping so much.

"When we've spoken to you, you've made it very clear that you didn't know Gabby very well," her eyes locked on his, "you made it seem like you had nothing to do with her, or nothing to do with this game Hito. We then found out that you did in fact play Hito, and that the last account to speak to Gabby belonged to you. We have additional new-found evidence that you were more interested in Gabby than you have led us to believe. How did you get your hands on this diary?"

The room had no windows. There was nowhere to look apart from the grey walls or the individuals at the other side of the table. The light above gave definition to every eye movement. Every face change. With nothing else to focus on, he stared into DCI Binyon's eyes. PC Gables tapped the tip of the fountain pen.

"We need an answer."

Ryan had always respected authority. He remembered how scared he used to get when he'd steal an iced lolly from the freezer and hoped that his dad didn't realise. He hated being told off by authority figures. So much so, that it kept him on track. At least it kept him on track until this investigation started. He could never before have imagined contemplating what he said next.

"No comment."

He bit his lip. Would they now have a target on his head?

PC Gables scribbled something onto his notepad, the tip of the pen making a satisfying etching sound like a calligraphist.

DCI Binyon slouched back into her chair.

"As someone of interest, you don't have to assist us with our investigation if you don't want to. It could, however, be very beneficial for you to tell us how you acquired this diary, for this girl you didn't know very well. You wouldn't want to look suspicious, after all."

The greyness of the room now matched the colour of Ryan's face. His insides hurt. He could feel sick snaking its way up his throat from his stomach. He didn't like this. He didn't want to be here.

"No comment again," he spat out.

How would he explain he broke into Gabby's room? Or the secret investigation he has been running. The sick was still snaking its way up his pipe.

"Okay. There is something else we want to talk to you about. The relationship between your dad and Lorraine. Gabby was aware of this, and your dad frequently visited their house. You didn't find out this news until recently. One could assume that potentially Gabby told some people at school, and that this news may have got back to you much earlier than your parents are led to believe. Did you find out about this affair, and did it change how you viewed Gabby at all?"

He took a large breath in, readying himself for a reply. The taste of sick was now in his mouth. He put his hand over his mouth and closed his eyes. Gulping, he tried to force it back down.

"Ryan, are you okay?"

He waved his other hand to signal he was fine. The sick snaked its way back down his throat and he could feel the stench start to disappear. He was lucky this time. Opening his eyes, the room seemed brighter than before, and his tear ducts had filled up.

She stood up and PC Gables dropped his pen onto the notepad, another small leak joining the illegible scribbles on the page. She gestured for him to stand.

"We'll end this here then. You don't look well, and you're not giving us anything." He could tell she was displeased with him. She walked him back out of the interview room, and down the corridor, keeping a distance ahead. She stopped at the open door at the top. She leaned into him, and he was sure she must have been able to smell the potential sick.

"I know you know more than you say. Off the record, we're rapidly ruling out other people. We checked out Mr Dhanial after what you said last time. He was in Germany with his wife on the weekend of Gabby's disappearance. We have witnesses, as well as passport control confirming this. We're ruling out other persons of interest too. It won't be long until we are solely focusing on you. You need to start speaking soon."

The door slammed shut.

He stood in the reception, staring at the door, his stomach bubbling with unrest. He darted into the toilet and coughed up his entire insides.

Chapter 23

Detention

The humiliation returned when Ryan had to be driven back to school in a police car. This time by a different officer. He asked the man to pull over the street before school. The man didn't hear, or perhaps chose not to. The quiet classroom picked up a rustle when he walked in.

It was break at 2pm when Ryan felt the loneliest. He stood in the corner of the yard. It was overwhelming going through all of this in one day, especially as he didn't have Cali. The sickly smell still lingered in his throat, with the fear that it could return and build at any moment. He was sure he could hear whispers from groups around the yard as to why he was taken to the station.

A whoosh sound filled the air. Ryan turned his head and ducked just in time, the football missing him by an inch. The door behind thudded as the ball hit at full force. It dropped down and rolled between his legs and one of the football team came to collect it. He didn't bother apologising or acknowledging Ryan's existence.

After the survival instinct had subdued, he returned to thinking more about Gabby, the police, suspects and what he could hope to find from the Hito game makers in Sheffield. His eyes glazed over. Was he overlooking some information? He was so caught up in his thoughts that he didn't even see that Max and Cali were walking towards him.

Max was striding with purpose whilst Cali lingered behind.

"You didn't say anything," Max said throwing his voice a few metres from Ryan, "what do they know?"

Ryan lifted his head and looked blankly at Max, still half-entranced by his thoughts.

"What shouldn't I have said?"

"You know what...about me and Cali," Max whispered looking flustered.

Cali stood there awkwardly not looking directly at either of them.

"I didn't say anything."

Max nodded.

"Are you...still...you know...investigating?" Cali asked.

"No, I'm over that. I just want my life to be normal," he said as he pulled on his backpack straps.

"By the way, I've seen your name on the detention list for tonight. What's that about?" Max said.

Ryan's face smacked into comprehension as he remembered how Mr Dhanial had given him detention. He shuffled again with his straps.

"Erm...just a misunderstanding."

Max nodded and turned away, whilst Cali offered a familial smile before following across the yard. Cali always five paces behind to not arouse any accusations.

The door opened and Mr Moore stumbled out.

"Oh, sorry, I didn't see you there."

A whistle tied to string, bounced as he threw it down and it hit off his chest.

"You've got detention with me this evening so just come up to my classroom at the end of the day."

All the students flooded through the doors around the yard, heading to class with the end of break being marked by the blowing of the whistle. He stood there. Within moments, the yard was empty, and he was left alone again. The rest of the day sauntered on and his usual relief was replaced with a muted sigh.

He dragged himself up the three sets of stairs to Mr Moore's classroom. He peered through the window and saw him at his desk. He'd never had detention before. Grabbing the door handle, he strolled in. Mr Moore pointed to a seat in the first row.

"Just you and me tonight," Mr Moore said as he stared at his computer screen, "What did you get detention for anyway? You're not one of the usual suspects."

"Mr Dhanial caught me snooping in his office."

He hoped this would be the end of the conversation. That he'd be safe to sit in silence until the one-hour detention was up. He was wrong.

"Well, I best not leave the room otherwise you'll be snooping on my desk." He let out a deep laugh. "What were you looking for?"

He didn't want this. This was opening a can of worms he didn't need. He had to protect his investigation.

"Just being nosey I guess."

"And what did you find?"

Ryan's face melted as he stared at Mr Moore. His eyes were locked onto him like an eagle.

"Not much. I found out he played a game and that's about it. Nothing too interesting."

"A game, ha? Is it Hito?"

"Yeah. Have you heard of it?"

"It's hard not to when you teach kids day in, day out. They're always chattering about the latest craze," he said picking up a piece of chalk.

Ryan knew what was coming and he winced before the chalk had hit his lips.

"Sir, can I ask you a question?"

Mr Moore looked back at Ryan.

"Is your name Bob?"

"Yes," he said as the right side of his face twitched, "What business is it of yours? I think you best be quiet until your detention finishes. You don't want to be getting another one for asking teachers about their personal lives."

His fingers thumbed the keyboard for the rest of the time. He grunted at Ryan to signal the end of the detention. As he was leaving, he heard Mr Moore's phone ring.

"Hurry up and get out," Mr Moore shouted as Ryan dawdled.

The walk home was different. He didn't take in any of the surroundings, any of the people passing by. Nor notice the husky that was pulling its small owner along at rapid speed.

Instead, he thought. Over and over in his mind he was replaying the police interview. Thinking about what the police would think of him for giving no comment to the questions. He wondered how long he would have until they made him an official suspect. Had Gabby's DNA matched the body found in Robins Wood? Was Mr Dhanial's alibi as solid as the police said, and if so, who was Tino6000?

Chapter 24

Homecoming

He reached the front door and twisted the key into the lock. As soon as it opened, Mum rushed to him.

"I'm so sorry son," she said, tears streaming down her face, "I wish I could have been at the station with you. I still don't know why that bloody Lorraine was in your room to start with." Her hands were trembling as she held them out to him, stains all over her clothes from her cleaning shift.

"It's okay mum. It was all okay at the police station. I'm fine."

She stepped back and smiled at him. A door opened upstairs, and he heard his dad rushing down.

"You're back. Are you okay?" Dad shouted from the stairwell.

Ryan shouted back that he was fine, and Dad came down the stairs.

"What did you say to the police? Why did you have her diary?"

His mum tutted. "Why do we have to get into all this now. Let's just give Ryan a break."

She was right – he didn't want to talk about it. He really appreciated his mum looking out for him.

"But what about Lorraine? She's upstairs worrying about what could have happened."

"Well, you can tell Lorraine, to piss off out of this house. And for once you can start caring about this family and your son."

Dad's jaw hit the floor. He was clearly shocked at what she said. Ryan couldn't help but smirk. Mum grabbed onto Ryan's hand, and they walked into the sitting room. They sat down on the sofa, and she grabbed a cushion for her lap.

"Some good news – I got the full-time cleaning job I interviewed for!"

Ryan leapt up and hugged his mum. He knew how much this meant to her.

Dad entered the living room and saw them both embracing. He looked awkward until him and Mum were sitting back on the sofa.

"It's not easy for me. And I know my priorities might have been off recently," Dad said with a stutter, "but I want you both to know that I do care for you. And I am sorry for how I've been recently."

Ryan knew this was very big for his dad. He could count on his fingers how many times he had apologised in the past. He got up from the sofa and hugged him, before his mum joined them too.

"I love you both so much, and nothing will ever change that."

The three of them had a very pleasant, almost normal, happy dinner. It could have been a Christmas advert for how perfect it looked to an outsider. Lorraine weirdly refused to come downstairs. At one point they heard the front door shut, signalling that she must have left the house.

With time to kill this evening, he went up to his room and switched on the computer to load up Hito. The loading bar seemed to take an eternity. The ominous music hadn't kicked in, so he was sitting in silence staring at the screen. At last, it loaded.

He found himself in the chatroom where he last found Tino6000. There were a lot of people in this time. He moved his cursor from hito to hito scouting who was in there tonight. The same non-descript names stood out. Fake names galore. Ernestsmith. That wasn't someone's name who lived in Thurlcaster, and certainly not someone young enough to play Hito.

He sped up his cursor as pairings would likely be made very soon. They were still all names he didn't recognise. His cursor hit the next person and as soon as he read the name, he recognised it. Her name read gabbymcgee. Was she alive? His fingers thinking fast typed CTRL + 7 onto the keyboard and then typed in her username. He needed to have a connection session with her.

There were so many questions. If it wasn't her, it could have been her abductor, murderer, who knows.

The connection session began. The ominous music slipping through the speakers as his anticipation grew. It loaded. His hito was standing outside of a white lighthouse. It was night with darkness encompassing everything. The lighthouse slowly spun 360 degrees, and as it did it would illuminate everything within its path.

As it hit the sea, he could see a cargo ship heading towards the shoreline. It let out a deep trumpeted sound as it beckoned closer to the cliffside. Seagulls flew overhead each time the horn sounded, crying out their own calls. As the light passed the grassy bank to his left, an isolated wooden hut sat still. The light going straight through the windows, revealing the dusty cobwebs.

Walking over to the hut, he examined the outside to see if there was a way for his hito to step inside. Perhaps Gabby's hito was in there. The door had a padlock placed on the front. He stood next to the window, and waited for the lighthouse to pass so he could see inside fully. The illuminated beam shone through, and all was revealed for a moment. An old red chair sat by itself opposite a fireplace. That was all. There was no other hito inside.

He walked back to the lighthouse. The door was now open at the bottom. He stepped into the circular foyer and ascended the twirling narrow staircase. They winded up as far as the eye could see.

The last few stairs allowed him to see the main floor. The giant bulb sat in the middle. He walked around the planked area surrounding it. There was no one here either. Where was Gabby? The sea roared beneath him and as the beam struck the cargo ship, he realised there was a figure standing at the front of it. It was very close to approaching the dock. It was her.

He ran down the forever spindling stairs until he reached the bottom, and then scaled a wooden platform staircase which he'd missed before. It led from the cliff down to the dock. Only a flash of light every now and then highlighted his path.

The ship was docked. Not being able to wait any longer, he typed "Gabby" onto the keyboard so she could see it was him. He didn't get a response. He reached the dock and ran right to the end where the ship was anchored. She was descending a metal staircase that had been attached to the dock from the ship. He scrolled his mouse over her hito now he was close enough. Abbigailfitzgerald. It was a different hito.

The connection pairing cheat hadn't worked this time. Or had he just imagined her username? He angrily pressed exit on the screen with Hito vanishing. It had been a waste of time.

He looked back up at the now empty screen to see a yellow flashing icon at the bottom. This must have been Cali apologising again. He opened the window and read the message.

Thurl123: *I warned you. Stop the investigation. You carried on. The police have Gabby's diary. If the police don't put you in prison soon, I'll make sure you're next on my list. From, The Person You Won't Find.*

His heartrate palpable. His hand fell off the mouse and hit his lap.

Walking over to the hatch, he pulled up the ladder and loaded it until it clicked in place. Nobody could hurt him here, and he'd be ready to find the answers he needed tomorrow.

Chapter 25

Dyme St

The bus rattled along the M1. Ryan had tucked himself into a window seat on the middle of the bus. A man loudly chewed on sweets next to him. Ryan grimaced with each sweet that swirled its way around his mouth. He pulled up his backpack from beneath his legs and looked in it for the fifth time.

A two-litre bottle of Evian water. An atlas filled with maps of the UK which he stole from his dad's car. A book to read for his journey; 'A Series of Unfortunate Events: The Bad Beginning' (he quickly realised however he wouldn't be able to concentrate on anything else).

He wondered what he'd say when he got to 32 Dyme Street. How cooperative would they be to speak? If they had kidnapped Gabby, they wouldn't think twice about doing the same to him too.

A scene where he would confront them, and karate chop them to the floor rolled in his head. And then a scene where he pulls out a gun and threatens to shoot unless they give him answers. And then they would start running and the police would close in at the same time, with the police thanking Ryan for leading them to the true criminals and solving the case.

All these situations he knew were unlikely and instead what you'd see in a film.

He was also thinking about the most peculiar sight that he'd seen whilst waiting at the bus station. Max was cycling ferociously past, and it looked like he was heading into the industrial part of the town. Where the factories and manufacturing plants were.

If he didn't have this bus to catch, he would have attempted to chase after him and see where he was going. There was nothing for a fourteen-year-old in that part of town.

The whole bus jerked forward as the bus screeched to a brake. An accident ahead had shut down the road. Police signalled traffic into a single lane. The bus crawled through the slow-moving traffic. Rationally he knew the police wouldn't notice that he was truanting, but he couldn't resist slumping down in his seat as the bus passed the policeman.

"Shouldn't you be at school?" the man next to him said with a sweet still swirling around in his mouth.

The man was right of course, it was a Tuesday. He had pretended to his mum that today was a normal day. He left the house dressed in his uniform with his school bag. Once he got to the bus station, he changed in the toilets before boarding. If he timed his return bus just right, he'd be back at home at the usual time. His parents wouldn't be any the wiser.

"Inset day," he replied to the man.

He shrugged and returned to his bag of sweets.

The bus pulled into the station and came to a sudden halt. Everyone stood up and dragged their bags out from the overhead storage. The man next to him stayed seated, trapping Ryan. After all other passengers had got out, he stood up and slowly made his way off the bus, Ryan eagerly behind him the full way. He took a deep breath as he stood in the fresh air. The two-hour journey had seemed a lot longer.

Pulling out the atlas, he flicked to page 165 which was the map of Sheffield city centre. He'd already used a felt tip pen to mark out the route to take from the bus station. Twisting the atlas around, he tried to figure out his bearings.

He followed the map, twisting and turning the atlas whenever he thought it would help him understand it better. After fifteen minutes he reached the top of a road that read 'Dyke Street'. The covered up "m" had been replaced by some vandals with a "k." 'Not very funny,' Ryan thought to himself. At least he had found the street.

He continued down the road. All the even-numbered houses on the left-hand side. 32 shimmered in gold letters on the front of the worn door. It was merely a terraced house, like what he lived in himself. Hito couldn't be based here. Cali must have located the address wrong, or they must be masking their server location. The curtains on the front window were closed and looked as if they hadn't been opened for years.

A frail woman emerged from the house next door. A walking stick in hand to support herself. She paused and looked over at Ryan on the other side of the wall, squinting as she did.

"Sorry," he said taking his opportunity, "do you know who lives there?"

She looked away from him and at the gold number glimmering on the door. Her eyes blinking a few times as she did. She hobbled with her walking stick a few paces and then looked back over.

"Trouble. That's who." She continued her frail walk down the street.

Ryan knocked once on the door and took a step back. His breath catching up with itself. A loud squeak of the floorboards indicated that someone was on the other side. The peephole in the centre of the door changed colour. Someone was looking at him. He heard the floorboards squeaking again. The person had left the door and was walking away.

He was adamant to speak to them. He knocked three times on the door, each knock louder than the last. The squeakiness returned. What must have been a chain rattled the other side as the door slithered open slightly.

"Hello?" Ryan said.

"What do you want?" a harsh male voice said.

"I want to talk...about Hito," Ryan asked with a nervous tone flowing through his voice. He didn't know what to expect.

"What's Hito?"

"It's a game. I thought you may have been the creator."

"I'm not, sorry."

"No worries," Ryan took another pace back from the door, "my friend is missing, and she played Hito. I've travelled two hours and I was hoping you would be able to help me. I must have been wrong."

He turned around and walked out the gate, his head flung to the ground in disappointment. The chain rattled once more, and Ryan assumed the door must have closed fully.

"Wait," the voice called out.

Chapter 26

Elliot

The door was now fully open. A man in his early twenties stood there in a grey hoodie. His hair mouse-brown, wavy and messy. He wore the same style glasses as Ryan.

Ryan took a few cautious steps, and a heavy feeling consumed him as he stepped into unknown territory. The hallway had a myriad of wires running across the floor and scaling the walls. Red. Blue. Green. Yellow. It was almost impossible to avoid standing on them. He ushered Ryan into the living room.

A battered black leather sofa lay against the wall, where he sat down, leaning forward so he was ready to bolt at any moment. With the curtains drawn and no lights on, the room was surprisingly light. Eight computer screens were lined up against the walls. One had the Hito homepage. One had a rolling leaderboard with the names constantly morphing. The remaining all had what looked to be blue screens of code.

The last computer screen sitting directly opposite him caught his attention. On this was the news article about Gabby disappearing. Her image smiling back at him.

"So, your friend has gone missing. Is this her?" He pointed at the computer screen. His fingernail was exceptionally long, covering the top half of Gabby's image.

Ryan nodded taking a big gulp. The man took a few steps closer to him.

"You don't have to be scared," he whispered, "you're safe here."

His skin crawled at those words. He shouldn't have come to this house. If he went missing now, nobody would know where he was. Max didn't see him standing at the bus stop this morning when he cycled manically. His parents would think he was at school as normal.

"Please don't kill me," he blurted out like a cough.

The man took a few steps closer and sat down next to him on the sofa. The man's leg gently grazed against Ryan.

"I'm not going to kill you. Did you not hear what I just said?"

"Well, you're acting strange. A normal person doesn't have to say they're not going to kill you." His breath louder as the backpack viced between his legs.

"Sorry, I don't get out much. That could be why."

"Oh…" Ryan said.

"I've always been an outcast. 'Elliot Smelliot' they called me at school. You don't think I smell, do you?"

Ryan laughed. "No, and I'm an outsider too."

"Sorry to hear about your friend. So, your name is…?"

"Ryan. I'm Ryan Jones."

Elliot's face dropped as he heard the name.

"I'm so sorry. The police forced me to hand over your Hito account. I didn't want to." An honesty flowed from Elliot's voice.

The glasses, the messy hair. It was in a way like he was looking in a mirror.

"Have you given them the conversations I had on Hito?" he said barely able to contain himself.

"No, that wouldn't be possible. I don't store conversations; they're all encrypted. The police have come to me a few times looking for different pieces of information. They're mostly concerned with you and a Tino1000."

"Tino6000! And what did you give them?"

"There was nothing to give them. The email address was a dummy."

Ryan scratched his head. Tino knew what they were doing from the outset. They wanted to remain anonymous. He told Elliot all about his investigation; about how he wanted to find the person who took Gabby. He told him how he thought Mr Dhanial could have been the owner of the Tino6000 account but how he had a watertight alibi.

"You know, it crossed my mind that you may have kidnapped Gabby, if I'm being completely honest," Ryan said looking down at the floor.

"Why would you think it was me? You didn't even know me?"

"Hito is a crazy game. All of the little tricks like being able to switch someone's webcam on. Operating a creepy phone line where you can buy buki?"

Elliot stood up next to him and placed a hand on his shoulder, letting out a small laugh as he did.

"Oh boy. I guess it's my turn to be interviewed. Where do I start? I had the idea of Hito when I was fourteen years old. I wanted to create a game where kids could connect with others in their area. Somewhere I wouldn't be seen as Elliot Smelliot."

"I get that."

"In Hito, I wanted to create a world where people are rewarded for meaningful exchanges. Of course, free-will plays a big part of the game. Intensely bullying someone is rewarding, but equally loving messages and actions earn a lot of buki too. As long as it's deep exchanges, you're rewarded."

"Ahhhhhhh," Ryan let out.

"Unfortunately, as the game got more popular, people have exploited it. That weird webcam trick wasn't built into the game. That was a hacker. I'm still scouring to find that line of code and delete it."

"Oh god, I hope you find it. Why do all of this yourself? Just hire someone? Run an office?"

Elliot laughed. "Oh kiddo, when you get older, you'll realise it's not that easy. I make zero money from the game."

"What? But the buki phoneline? You must make a fortune from that?"

"Another hack unfortunately. Trying to find that line of code too."

"Oh...sorry Elliot."

Elliot sat down in the swivel computer chair. A poster sat on the wall behind. Across the top "Hito" was scrawled in the now infamous font style, and below a picture of a hito which was clearly Elliot's. That must have been the first ever hito.

"It all makes sense now," Ryan said. He was saddened that he couldn't get the answers that he had wanted.

"Is there anything else you can do to help me find Gabby?"

"Hmmm," he said swivelling in the chair, "I don't think so. We know who Gabby communicated to on the game. Mainly you and Tino6000. I don't store chat conversations and Tino6000 has a dummy email account so we can't confirm their identity."

"How about we find him the same way I found you. Do you store the IP address of users?"

"I do," he swivelled around and faced one of the computer screens. "You should work in the police. They've not thought of this."

He typed some code into the screen, and the blue hue changed to different shades. The words constantly changing with code running down the screen like rain. He then typed in Tino6000. The IP appeared. He loaded up an IP checker site and dropped it in there.

"It looks to be in Thurlcaster."

Ryan leaped up from the sofa and rushed to the desk. Thurlcaster was no surprise.

"But where exactly is the question?"

He leaned over Elliot's shoulder and looked at the map on the screen. He recognised the location immediately. He'd walked past many times before. In fact, he saw Max cycling in that direction this morning. It was on the outskirts of the town in the industrial epicentre. The abandoned Hoverton bread factory on Wessington Way.

He thought that nobody had been in that place for years. At least it didn't look like it from the outside.

"You're not going to go there, are you?" Elliot said staring at him.

"Of course. I need to find out the truth."

After looking down at his watch, he rushed back over to the sofa and threw his backpack over his shoulder.

"Thanks Elliot. You have my email. Let's keep in touch," he said as he headed out the door. Accidentally stepping on some of the wires in the frenzy.

Elliot shouted from the doorway, "Ryan, don't go there by yourself. It might not be safe."

The bus set off from the station heading back to Thurlcaster. He was luckier on the return trip and had the seat next to him free. No annoying sweet eating this time. Opening the atlas, he flicked through to Thurlcaster. He grabbed the felt tip pen and drew a line from the bus station to where the abandoned factory was on Wessington Way.

The bus pulled up into Thurlcaster station at 4pm. He didn't hang around, jumping down the steps and pulling out his map. He knew exactly where he was walking to. He found a comfort though in holding onto something, even if his eyes didn't need to look down at it. The path twisted behind the bus station and through a few residential streets. The trees lined the road as the sun still shone high in the sky.

He didn't have much of a chance to think through what he was going to find. If there would be anything at all, or a dead end. This part of town has a definitive partition, where the red brick from the houses transforms into the concrete from the factories. A grassy field separates both.

Each plot similar to the naked eye. A grey slab of concrete stretched across a vast amount of land. A meshed metal fence reached for 3 metres, with security cameras dotted along the route. Each factory creating something different on the inside. One building with an apple rising high on a flagpole out front, another the logo of a famous car brand. And then he reached it. The abandoned Hoverton bread factory.

He could remember his parents driving him past this place as a kid. Each space in the car park was filled, with people coming in and out of the metal front door. The smell of fresh bread drifting through the air.

He looked at the plot now. No cars out front. The lines of the spaces had all but buried themselves into the ground. Weeds overgrown around the perimeter with deep long grass resembling a jungle either side. Rubbish collecting next to the fence. No smell of bread. Barbed wire ran along the top of the fence and the surprisingly still sturdy gate was locked. The lock looked brand new. A crisp shade of silver contrasted against the tired grey gate.

He walked to the right and scaled the full perimeter. Buried beneath a carrier bag with empty bottles of alcohol lay a rip in the fence. He rushed under. He ran to the back of the bread factory to take cover. He didn't want anyone seeing him here. The back was more derelict than the front. The jungle encompassed everything bar the small patio space directly outside the rear door of the building.

The metal rusted door was wide open, inviting further inspection. He slowly stepped forward and crossed the line into the building. His heart thumping as the unknown took charge.

Dust particles floated like ghosts in the night. A mammoth conveyor belt ran the length of the room. It must have been off for many years. A rat scurried across the floor at the other side of the room. To his right, a metal staircase ran into the ceiling.

He carefully took one step at a time, gently resting his hand on the rail running up the stairs. With each step a small clunk rang around the room. He put his other hand over his mouth so his heavy breathing wouldn't be noticed.

As he reached the top he was greeted with darkness. There were no windows to the external world. He felt suffocated. Each breath shallower than the last. He pulled out his flip phone and shone it onto the ground. It looked to be a corridor of rooms. The first floorboard squeaked as he stepped onto it. Something scurried past him in the darkness. He jumped and let out a small gasp before forcing his hand back over his mouth.

He walked past the first two doors, his phone still poorly lighting the way. The light as good as a firefly on a lead. The floorboard behind him squeaked. He turned around to see what it was. Something pushed his arm.

His phone flew across the room, lighting just a far corner of the corridor. A silhouette stood before him. A heavy breath hit his eyelids. He screamed as loud as he could. Then...darkness.

Chapter 27

Wessington

"Ouch."

He tried to raise his hand to his head. He couldn't. Again. Still no movement. A pain shot through his wrists, and he realised they were tied behind him.

His eyes were blurry, he could only make out vague shapes as he looked around the room. He'd never felt so helpless in his life. In front there was a desk with a computer. Hito was loaded on the screen with a character standing there. His eyesight still not good enough to make out who it was. A bright light was rattling above his head, making him squint as he tried to peruse the environment. What looked like filing cabinets lined the wall to the left of him. Some had their drawers pulled out with papers covering the floor.

Squinting his eyes harder through his glasses, he looked back at the computer screen. The character was Tino6000. A metallic jumpsuit. He shuffled his wrists in his chair, but they were too tightly bound. His legs, which he hadn't noticed to this point, were also strapped solidly to the metal chair. It was nailed to the floor. He had no way out.

The clock that had read 8pm with his fuzzy eyes, now read 9.20pm clearly. If it wasn't for the harsh synthetic lighting, the room would be enveloped in darkness. He twisted his head around to examine the rest of the room behind him. Another desk with another computer but this one was switched off. A small radio sat upon the desk with the aerial tilted towards the sky. A printer jammed into the corner of the room with a red light on the front. A dust sheet tucked under the desk.

Heavy footsteps got louder along the corridor outside. The floorboards felt like they were closing in on him. The grey door which was the only way in or out had a square window in the top of it, with a pane of distorted glass. It reminded him of what you'd see on a bathroom window. He hoped the squeak of the floorboards would be that of a rat scurrying. He knew that was too optimistic. The floorboards sounded closer and closer. And then a figure appeared through the tainted glass. They were here. He imagined Max standing there.

The doorknob turned. Ryan's heartrate running a marathon. The figure stepped through the doorway and revealed themselves into full view. The light shining on them. Even without the chalk grappled in his hand, Mr Moore stood as firmly to the ground of this factory as he did within the classroom. He didn't know what to say. He never expected it to be him. It was supposed to be Max. He stepped closer to Ryan.

"You can call me Bob here," he said with a smile on his face.

He walked over to the computer and sat down slowly into the chair.

"Well did you," he paused for a heavy breath, "did you expect it to be me that was Tino6000?" His eyes super focused on Ryan.

Ryan shook his head. He realised he made a grave mistake coming here. He should have gone straight home. Was Mr Moore going to kill him? Had he already killed Gabby? The pain of the restraints erupted from his wrists and rippled all the way up to his chest.

"Why would you think it was me? You followed my card and saw the Tino account loaded onto Saj's computer. He was the perfect distraction for you. And for the police for a while."

That's why he recognised the handwriting. He saw it on the blackboard each English Literature lesson. Ryan closed his eyes and willed himself to be anywhere else. He reopened them and he was sad to see that he was still there. Mr Moore spun his chair around to face the computer.

"You best get comfortable, you'll be here for a while."

"No, I won't," Ryan shouted. Bob twisted around in shock. "I told Cali where I was going. He'll tell the police when I don't contact him soon and then they'll come and arrest you."

He laughed, undoing the top button of his shirt.

"I know you're not friends with Cali anymore. I know you two had a falling out. I'm sure you haven't told anyone, which means I can keep you here until the right moment."

He faced the computer again. Ryan could feel himself about to cry; he didn't want to show weakness even to the back of him. He pursed his lips together and tried to shun any tears from appearing. He had to be brave. Now was the time he had to fight for himself.

"I should have realised it was you," Ryan said as Bob turned back around. The connection session had now loaded onto the screen with bubbles appearing over the other hito's head.

"I heard that there was a creepy teacher playing Hito and I should have put two and two together. It was obviously you."

Mr Moore grinned.

"What did you do to Gabby?" Ryan clenched his teeth together as if they were a fist.

Bob stared at him for a moment and then on the next ping of the speech bubble, turned back to face the screen. He couldn't make out what he was typing but no doubt it was lies. Pretending to be a child in Thurlcaster. The heavy breathing supplied a dark rhythm for the room. The odd snigger would surprise the room after a message would pop up and Ryan would jump. He wanted to be out of here. The screen faded blue, and the connection session ended. Bob got up from his chair and switched off the monitor. He slinked over to Ryan.

"My work for today is done. It's almost 10pm. Time for you to sleep. Don't forget your supper first."

He pulled out a piece of white chalk from his right hand and stuffed it into Ryan's mouth. The gritty texture hitting his lip and collapsing onto his tongue. The dry taste filling up his tastebuds. He coughed and spat it onto the floor.

"Go to hell, you creep."

Bob switched off the light before slamming the tinted door behind him. He was there. Alone. In the dark. The residue of the chalk still on his tastebuds. He gagged trying to get the taste from his mouth. His eyes couldn't adjust to this level of darkness. There was nothing. Ideas raced through his mind of what Mr Moore's agenda was. Was he using Hito to kidnap kids?

He couldn't see the time on the clock, or even the clock itself for that matter. He lost track and his thoughts became his reality. He saw himself sitting at the dinner table with his mum and dad. Lorraine was there too. As well as Gabby. They were laughing at a joke he'd just told. Mum was working her new full time job and supporting herself. Lorraine and Dad were living together and would come around with Gabby every Friday night. Life was different to before; it would never be the same. But they were all as happy as they could be.

He must have dozed off. When he awoke, there was a slither of light climbing in through the bottom of the doorway from the corridor. 2.15am the clock read. He wondered how long he'd be here for. He wondered what Bob's plan would be for him. Would it be whatever his plan was with Gabby?

The whites of his eyes squinted to try to stay open. And then he fell asleep again. He was like a parrot in a cage with a blanket atop. He couldn't stay awake when it was this dark. A loud thud from downstairs awoke him for the final time. It could have been anything. Someone else breaking in. The police may have found him. He kept visualising DCI Binyon at the door, ready to set him free. The rustle continued up the tinny aluminium stairs and the squeaks of the floorboard at the top of the corridor. This time the sounds were different. He heard wheels scraping along the floor.

A figure appeared through the frosted glass, and he prayed that it was someone here to save him. The door swung open, and the heavy breath and chalky hands of Mr Moore stomped into the room. Ryan sighed. Moore glanced him up and down, and walked around him examining that the rope restraints were still in-tact. He then disappeared back out into the hallway. He looked back up to the door when he saw Mr Moore coming back in. He was speechless. The wheels were attached to a chair. But the surprising thing was who sat within the chair.

Her blonde hair tossed over the chair that she was slumped within. Her arms pinned back, similar to Ryan, and her face expressionless. Her eyes closed. Her makeup smudged from weeks of being here. Her Ugg boots sagging and scuffed. She was alive though.

"We need to keep you in here," Mr Moore said pushing her over to face the back of Ryan. He heard a jangle and tried to turn his head around, to which he saw Bob holding up a pair of handcuffs. Ryan tried shaking his hands to stop Mr Moore but to no avail. The sharp click snapped in the air. His left wrist was tighter, a weight dropping his arms further down the chair which caused a pain in his shoulders.

"There you go. Now neither of you are going anywhere."

Ryan's eyes looked like a doll as he watched him walk out the door and slam it shut. The room shivered behind him. With his fingers, he carefully stroked the palm of her hand. She was ice-cold.

"Gabby, are you okay? Can you hear me?"

Apart from his own heavy breath, not a single noise from her.

The clock was teasing him. Every minute that passed felt like an hour. He'd close his eyes and imagine that she had spoken.

He sat there still. Looking as expressionless as Gabby did when she was wheeled into the room. The handcuffs jangled. A song that he wasn't expecting to hear. And then a grunt as they jingled some more. The plastic of the wheeled chair moaned.

"Who are you?" she let out.

Chapter 28

The Pill

His back sharpened, raising the handcuffs. He wanted to be able to turn around and look into her eyes.

"It's Ryan...from school. Ryan Jones."

"Oh...Ryan," she replied with a dazed tone to her voice, "I'm so glad you're here." The handcuffs jingled. He imagined her eyes slowly starting to come back to life.

"I was looking for you. I was investigating your disappearance. And I found you. Except I was a bit stupid and now I'm trapped here too."

"Lets...just...try. We need to get out," she whispered.

He scanned the room assessing it for anything that could help them escape. The computer desk, printer, a radio and a dust sheet. Then there was the small issue that Ryan's chair was nailed to the ground. He wasn't going anywhere.

"Your chair is on wheels! He wheeled you in here! Your legs aren't restrained, are they? Just your hands tied to mine. Are you very flexible?"

She laughed. "I... don't think now is the time or place, Ryan." Her laugh was natural and pure. He could sense her coming back to herself. "Five years of forced Pilates classes, so yes."

"Can you bring your legs under yourself, like you're kneeling on the seat, and then push against the back of my chair? It might just be enough to break my chair from the ground and release the nails."

Ryan focused on the clock ahead of him. This way he wouldn't distract her. He also didn't want to risk twisting around and the restraints feeling tighter, making Gabby's job harder. He could feel Gabby stand up, or at least stand up the furthest she could whilst being handcuffed to him. She then lifted one foot from the floor, and shakenly tucked it under herself. Her foot hit the palm of his hand, creeping in through the back of the chair. The wheels on the chair dropped back to the floor as she placed her full bodyweight onto the chair. Her right foot touched his other hand.

Ryan's wrists were now deadweight. He was sympathetic for Gabby who must have been in her chains for much longer. With all his force, he lifted both of their hands up as high as he could, holding hers as gently as he could. The highest he could raise them was only a few inches from where they had been, but it was all that they needed.

"Can you push your feet on the back of my chair? Use all of your force and let's try to get these nails out."

Gabby arched her upper body and slid her feet backwards as they loudly hit the back of his metal chair. He could feel her pushing. The chair roared with each push she delivered. Ryan leaned forward pushing his weight in the same direction for extra force. The nails fixed below looked as secure as ever. With the sixth push, Gabby let out a scream.

"I can't do it anymore, it's not budging."

"Please Gabby," he pleaded, "We can do this. Just one more time." He held onto her hands tighter and felt her body shaking from the exhaustion.

She leaned again and pushed her legs as hard as she could. The chair once again groaned, and Ryan counterweighed with all of his force. He looked down and saw that all four of the nails on each leg were still solidly in place. He let out a whimper. Tears began streaming down his face. He couldn't hold it in. Gabby joined Ryan in crying, and he continued to hold her hands.

They sat still for a while, with whimpers and sniffles being the only sounds.

"Thanks for coming to find me. And...I'm sorry you're stuck here too. It should just be me here."

"Well," he stammered, "I wasn't very nice to you. The night you disappeared I said some awful stuff to you on Hito." She couldn't see him, but he sank his head shamefully. The clock ticked on the wall.

"Don't feel bad. I knew that was you. I saw your name and knew that your parents were separating so put it together. I'm just sorry for what I said in class."

She touched the palm of his hand, and he lifted his head back from the ground.

"So, what happened exactly? Why has Mr Moore done all of this to you?"

She sighed.

"You don't have to tell me." He stretched out his finger and gently caressed her palm.

"It's a long story," she took in a deep breath. "I always try to trick people on Hito with the webcam cheat. You know, switch on their webcam without them knowing."

"I know it too well," he said remembering his first encounter.

"Anyway, I did that with Tino6000 and saw that it was Mr Moore. How weird for a teacher to be on there!? I threatened to tell Mr Dhanial about him pretending to be a kid online. He completely flipped out and started offering lots of stuff. He said I would get better grades in English Lit if I kept it to myself. He also promised to get me into the leaderboard by gifting me buki."

"Oh," Ryan said.

"I didn't do the right thing. I wish I could have gone back and told someone. The Friday I went missing he went completely crazy in school. He pulled me to one side and searched my bag. He ripped apart so much of my diary. I was only left with a few entries. He promised to make it up to me that evening. He gave me a phone and said he'd text it with details of where I needed to meet him. I should have known I was walking into a trap. Stupid, stupid Gabby."

He was stumped. He didn't know what to say. The puzzle pieces were coming together. The ripped pages of the diary. Why Gabby mysteriously walked into the darkness of night. Mr Moore being missing from school, no doubt to continue with his secret double life as an abductor. She clung onto his finger like someone who knew that death was on the horizon.

"You're not stupid Gabby. He was a weirdo and you got caught up in it. Why was he chatting to students on Hito? That's the only thing I don't understand."

She shuffled in her seat, the wheels squeaking against the floor making a noise. "I don't even know. And no idea how he had so much buki."

They sat in silence with just the clock ticking for a few moments.

"I was stronger when I first got here you know. I actually made it out on my second night. If only someone had heard me scream before he dragged me back in."

"Wow. You're so strong Gabby. And you should be proud you nearly got out."

They sat there again in the silence. Ryan staring at the clock wondering how much time they would have left. Would this be their last day on earth? A large thud came from downstairs again.

"What was that?" Gabby panicked.

They held each other's hands tightly as they prepared for the worst. Both of their hands becoming warmer as they feared for what was to come. A bubble of heat radiated from their clasped hands. Closer and closer. The squeaky floorboards reached their loudest. His figure shone through the door. Mr Moore heavy-footedly stepped into the room. He slung a backpack onto the computer desk with a sharp crash. Gabby's cry was stifled as if she didn't want to be heard.

He smirked as he walked past Ryan and faced Gabby.

"Shhhh," he whispered.

Gabby leaned backwards into Ryan. He clasped her hands firmer. He couldn't turn his head around, but he imagined Bob would have tried to stroke her face.

"Now, now, now... be nice."

"Leave her alone. You're a monster," Ryan shouted as he continued to grip Gabby's hands.

He walked around and leaned in close to him. His heavy breathing louder than ever. He could smell whisky on him. Tiny droplets fell out of his mouth and onto Ryan's lap. He looked down in disgust.

"I think you'll find, I'm not a monster. You kids are." He stormed over to the computer desk and picked up his backpack. He rummaged to the bottom of the bag and then pulled out a small see through clip bag with two brown capsules inside. The size of the bag seemed to drown out the tiny pills. The murky brown colour made them look like a vitamin supplement your mum would force you to have.

"Do you know what these are," he said as he walked closer to Ryan, dangling the bag closer to his eyes. Tiny lines lay across the sides of the pills, and he stared trying to see if he could decipher anything from them.

"Headache tablets to get rid of a pain like you?" Ryan snarked.

"Not quite," Mr Moore grinned back. "It's called the L-Pill. One little bite on this brown capsule will release cyanide salts, killing you."

Chapter 29

Buki

Gabby's crying erupted. It was no longer stifled as she struggled to control herself.

"Please, don't do this to us."

"This is the best way to go. You won't feel a thing. Well not for long anyway." He laughed.

"You're a psycho."

"You see, I have no other choice. You found me out. In fact, you both found me out. I wasn't going to hurt anyone. I just needed to make more money. A teacher's salary is tuppence."

"How exactly are you making money? Wait - you're involved in the pay scam aren't you!? You're stealing money from kids and giving them buki in return. That's why you have so much buki. You greedy -."

"Yes. They don't pay us enough for all our hours. Lesson planning. Marking homework. Putting up with brats like you. I'm not the only one. A group of us running the scheme, all of us becoming richer day by day. Oh, how happy my mother was when I told her I'll be moving out."

"You still live with your mum? That's sad," Gabby said through her tears.

He glanced menacingly in her direction. "I hate kids. I hate kids. I hate kids. The only joy I get in the classroom is licking chalk and seeing you all repulse. You didn't think I enjoyed it?" Bob grabbed a piece of chalk from his pocket and threw it across the room, bouncing off the corner wall.

"It was only a matter of time before you would have told someone I was on Hito, Gabby. Max. Or that nitwit Tina."

"Just let us go. Please. We never said anything horrible about you," Gabby said with tears streaming down her face, "we won't say a word to anyone. We promise. Nobody else knows it's you behind all of this. Keep making your money."

He stood there, still looking at Ryan whilst she begged for them to be released. Her crying echoing around the room. Ryan locked eyes with him and tried to show no fear on his face. His body wincing on the inside. He had to pretend he wasn't scared.

"You should both be happy with your planned exit," he said putting the pills back into his pocket, "it's very hard to get your hands on these usually. Otherwise, you'd have been gone a long time ago Gabby." He walked towards the door and threw the backpack onto his shoulder.

"I'll be back soon to take care of you both." He slammed the door behind him, and they were left alone with Gabby's cries reaching fever pitch.

He was still holding her hands and could feel her trembling. He was worried that she'd faint from crying so much. She gripped onto him.

A ticking clock of gloom sat above their heads, with each strike of the pendulum taking them closer to their impending doom. Gabby had run out of tears and was now sniffling, with the occasional cough thrown in.

What were people saying at school? Had anyone noticed that he was missing?

"Ryan..." Gabby said in a hopeless voice, "there's something I want to tell you, if we're both going to die anyway." She gripped him.

"Yeah?" he tried to twist his head as far as he could.

"I always liked you. Even when we played together when we were kids."

"I've always liked you as a friend too."

"I mean..." she hesitated, "as more than a friend."

How could someone like Gabby ever feel like this for him. The prettiest girl at Castle Montgomery. He didn't know what to say.

"I've always fancied you too. I wish we could spend more time together."

The Gabby in her diary was real. This was her. Sitting behind him. Holding his hand. He wanted to stay with this Gabby. He wanted to spend more time with this Gabby.

A few hours had passed, and the clock struck 7pm. It felt depressing to know he'd been here for 24 hours. A familiar thud sounded from downstairs. Was Mr Moore coming back to finish the job now? The metal stairs clanked as they had before, and the floorboards creaked. Closer and closer they got until the familiar silhouette appeared at the door. He stared at the silhouette with hate running through his body. He readied himself to be disgusted at the sight of Mr Moore as he opened the door. Gabby was lucky that she was facing the other way. The door opened halfway, and Ryan hung his head so he wouldn't have to look at him. He stared at his lap.

"Ryan! Gabby!" a voice said. This wasn't the slithering voice of Mr Moore. He lifted his head up and saw Max standing there. His blonde locks shimmering. His tall slim physique looking down on them.

"MAX!" Gabby shouted, "Is that you?"

Max ran to hug Gabby. Max's arms rubbed against him as he hugged her.

"What are you doing here? How did you find us?" she said.

"Well, I found you both...I had a feeling you may have been in this building." He fiddled with the handcuffs that joined them both together.

"How could you possibly guess that?" Ryan said. Max still fidgeting with the handcuffs.

"Out of all the buildings...you guessed that we were in this one? And why didn't you come here long before now? Gabby has been here for over 2 weeks. You knew I was trying to find where she was."

Max paused, his face turning a pale shade of red. His eyes couldn't focus on Ryan, instead preferring to look at the handcuffs in-between them.

"Max?" Gabby said.

He stayed looking down, fidgeting with his hands. He let out a sound from his mouth, as if he was going to talk, and then closed his mouth tight shut.

"Come to think of it, it's pretty odd that Mr Moore knew that me and Cali had fallen out. It's also weird that he knew that I was doing an investigation. You gave Lorraine the idea to look in my room and find the diary, didn't you. Mr Moore couldn't have planted that card at Tina's party either. That was you. You're working with Mr Moore."

Gabby gasped. Ryan could feel Gabby leaning closer to him for safety.

"You've come here to tease us. Get out and leave us alone."

Max dropped his hands to his side and let out a deep breath.

"I wasn't working with him, but I was giving him information."

"MAX! You've helped him do this," Gabby shouted.

"It's not what it seems...he was blackmailing me. He found out my secret and made me give him information about students in class. He wanted to know all the ins and outs of what Cali told me about your investigation. But he asked about everyone. What the classroom gossip was that week, who was dating who, you name it he wanted it. He bombarded me. Each time I'd refuse, he told me he would leak that I'm gay."

"You're gay!?" Gabby said. Max slowly nodded at her with a glint in his eye. "Well that makes a lot of sense now."

"I started to get suspicious. He gave me that envelope. I saw my chance and put it in the box then gave Cali the idea to look in there. I couldn't read it. It was sealed shut. He said to me that the police would suspect me, and that I should tell Lorraine to look in your room," he paused whilst he looked around.

Both Gabby and Ryan intently staring at Max.

"I started thinking more about the possibility of Mr Moore being the culprit. I cycled after him yesterday morning and tried to see where he was going. I lost him when he hit the industrial town. I did the same early this morning and followed him here. I had to leave for school to make it not look obvious that I was onto him."

He raised his hands to his face and started crying. "I'm so sorry, I didn't know that he had you, Gabby. Honestly. I didn't want this to happen to either of you. I would have just let it come out if I knew he'd use the information to do this." He was uncontrollable. His face flaming red and his skin blotched.

"And does Cali know Mr Moore was blackmailing you?"

"NO! I couldn't get him caught up in this. What if he started blackmailing him too." Max continued to cry covering his face.

"Okay, shut up and try to get us out," Ryan interrupted as Max peeked through his hands, "We need these off now. Then we can get emotional later."

He lifted the handcuffs that bound him and Gabby together. Max rushed over and tugged them. He pulled them apart which made them feel tighter. Max ran over to the desk in front of Gabby, looking for any signs of a key.

A familiar sound signalled danger. A thud from downstairs as the metal door must have opened. All three of them twisted their heads. It must be Moore returning. They would only have a few minutes before he would be up here. And if Max didn't get out, Mr Moore would have a third victim.

Chapter 30

The Game

They all stared at each other speechless with long faces.

"I'll be back soon," Max said opening the only door out.

"No!" Ryan shouted, "we need to tell someone where we are. Send a message on your mobile."

He patted his trouser pockets. "I don't have it on me."

Ryan glanced at the clock. There wasn't much time. His eyes looked down and onto the computer below. The game got them stuck here and it could be their way out.

"Switch on the screen. Go start a connection session on Hito," Ryan said nodding his head to the computer frantically. Max flew across the room and tapped the keyboard and mouse. Ryan was sure that Max was pressing more buttons than he needed to. The usual chatroom loaded, with a dozen hitos standing in the waiting area. Speech bubbles popped up. Max started typing but before he could press, the pop up appeared, and Max swiftly clicked yes to accept the session.

"Oh god, I hope it starts soon. You better have a plan B mate, otherwise we're all toast."

The loading bar appeared whilst the American voice came from the speakers.

Ryan's face was frozen, his eyes fixed on the computer screen. Mr Moore ascended the metal staircase, each footstep was another thud to the ice cold metal.

"Welcome to Hito. You'll shortly be paired up with another hito..."

Max turned the speakers off.

"Hurry up," Gabby whispered, shuffling around in her seat.

Ryan glimpsed back at the clock, each second that the hand moved was a second closer to their fate. The footsteps sounded like they were nearing the top of the stairs, with the thuds getting louder.

The blue screen changed and Tino6000 was sitting in a bistro. A typical American-style coffee shop that you'd see in a movie.

"Twist – turn – pan - the mouse. Hurry! Look around!" Ryan said.

Max swivelled the mouse around and a figure was standing behind the counter in an apron. Her purple hair was visible enough for Ryan to see from this distance.

"Type the address and say we need help. Hoverton Bread. Wessington Way. Thurlcaster. That's it."

Max rapidly typing, his fingers could have had flames coming off them. Each button he pressed harder than the last. This was their SOS call.

"I'm panicking," he said as he typed. He took his fingers off the keyboard and looked at the screen and then pressed enter, "Done."

"Now type the words 'I'll show you my face.' Type those words exactly, Max." He couldn't make out if Max typed those words, but he saw the camera on top of the screen illuminate with a red light. The footsteps were coming down the corridor. Louder and louder. He knew that the camera box wouldn't appear on their screen, just on the other hito's.

Ryan let out a sigh of relief. At least someone beyond the three of them now knew their whereabouts.

"Now, hide!" Ryan said.

The floorboards creaked. Mr Moore must only be a few metres away from the door. He could open it at any moment.

He remembered when he tried to switch on Mr Moore's webcam, and he only had an audio link.

"Wait. Max, see if there's any tape covering the camera lens."

Max swooped back across the room and dug his fingers into the lens. A satisfying rip as he removed two chunks of tar-black tape. He scrambled to put the camera back onto the top of the monitor, the red light still silently illuminated. Whoever was on the other side would be able to see them now. He swiftly turned the screen off.

Max ran to the desk facing Gabby and pulled the dust sheet from under it. He slid it onto his back like a cape and then buried himself under the desk.

The door flew open, and the portly figure stood there threateningly. He slung his backpack onto the desk in his usual grunted manner, the bag sliding over the keyboard and pressing buttons along the way. He grumbled and walked over to Ryan. He smiled back at him. Ryan couldn't contain his relief at the prospect of being rescued.

"What have you got to be happy for. You're going to be dead in a few hours." A few droplets of saliva trickled out of his mouth and hit Ryan's cheek. He curdled his face in disgust.

Mr Moore peered around the room. His eyes going from corner to corner. He didn't think to look behind himself. If he did, he would have seen the tiny red light feeding the image to the purple haired Hito. He approached the desk where Max was hiding. Had he spotted him? He reached down and pressed a button on the printer. The clunking sound of it turning on filled the room.

He stood at the desk, a small corner of the dust sheet hanging out. He seemed to stare at the black screen of the monitor and groaned. He reached down and pressed the button to turn it on. The black faded into colour slowly. Colours that were abstract began to merge into clarity and an image started to build on the screen. It came into focus like a jump scare in a horror film. Gabby gasped. It was a mirror reflection of the monitor the other side of the room. The counter. A purple haired girl standing there. There were bubbles where she had spoken now, but he couldn't make out what she had said.

Mr Moore shot his head around to the computer at the other side of the room. He swung his arms at his side and marched. He grabbed the camera with his hand, pulling the cable from the back of the computer. The tower fell over from the force. The screen fell into blackness. The girl gone.

"Max, get out!" Gabby shouted.

Max soared up from his hiding place and threw the dust sheet to the floor. Mr Moore turned on his heavy feet. He paced to block the door that Max was heading for. Mr Moore reached into his back pocket. He shot his hand forward and light shimmered on the object.

The pointed end glistened for all of them to see. It was a knife.

"You betrayed me. You should have just kept giving me information. Nobody is going to care that you're gay when you're dead."

He pointed the knife at Max. He stepped back a few paces as Moore guarded the only exit. Sweat dripping down from his forehead, and around the crease at the top of his stomach. Max's face ghostly pale.

"You've been caught," Ryan said, "that person on Hito knows our address and has seen us tied here. They would have called the police. The game is up. They know it's you. You won't get anything from harming us."

Mr Moore squinted at Ryan who was now sitting confidently in the chair. Or at least pretending to be confident. Hiding the fear from his face as he saw his image reflecting in the knife.

"You think that's going to work?" Mr Moore laughed. Ryan's shoulders collapsed an inch. "Who's to say that person even rang the police. And besides, I've still got time to get you away if they did. My car is just outside."

He slowly moved backwards, still pointing the knife, and grabbed his backpack with his other hand. He pulled out another pair of handcuffs.

"Put these on," he said throwing them over to Max, "and no funny business."

Max raised his arms and sank his left hand into the ring and clicked it shut. He then did the same with his right hand and fastened it until it clicked. His hands now restrained in front of himself.

"Push down all the way," Mr Moore said, "I want to see your wrists pale." Max pressed the handcuffs against his thighs and each ring clicked two more times.

"Owwwww," Max exclaimed in pain.

Moore still pointing the knife whilst he moved towards the two of them in their chairs. He stooped before Ryan and quickly cut off his leg restraints. Ryan stretched out his legs in front of him and tried to kick Moore but missed.

"Now you two stand up and sidestep away from your chairs."

Gabby and Ryan stumbled to their feet. Ryan could feel Gabby's body was weak from being tied up for two weeks. They both still faced opposite direction to each other, attached by the handcuffs joined together behind their backs. She had no energy to lift her arms when Ryan raised the handcuffs a little higher. They clunkily stepped right away from the chairs. He tightly wrapped his hands into hers.

They took another step and he fell backwards, falling onto Gabby. Both of them lying on the floor, she screamed out in pain. He quickly flipped over so she was lying on his back whilst his face was pinned to the cold floor.

"You're holding us up," Mr Moore said looking down at them, "we need to get out now." He lifted Gabby a few inches up and slipped the key into the handcuffs. He threw Gabby off Ryan, and then clipped them shut on Ryan's wrists. Max leaped from one side of the room onto Moore's back, the knife falling out of his hand and missing Gabby by just a few centimetres. He let out a mighty roar and used all his weight to throw Max against the wall. The wall cracked and plaster cascaded down. Max's eyes were closed as he lay slumped against the wall with the handcuffs still around his wrists.

"MAX. You've killed him," Gabby screamed.

"We need to leave." Moore pulled some rope from his backpack and picked up Gabby in one swoop. "You're so weak you probably don't need this. But better to be safe than sorry." He restrained her wrists behind her back. "Now we're going. If one of you dares do anything again..." he said pointing the knife at them, "...this will be going into you."

Chapter 31

Game Over

They got up from the ground, still weakened from their fights. They headed out, with Moore leading the way. Ryan glanced at Max unconscious against the wall and hoped he was alright. He could see his chest moving up and down.

They followed behind Moore, her legs groaning with every step she took. She hadn't stood up for weeks. They made their way out, and along the creaky wooden floorboards. He knew the pattern of which floorboards creaked like a sick familial tune.

Ryan and Gabby stood at the top of the staircase, whilst Moore raced down.

"Trust me. I'll keep us safe. We'll get out of this, okay?"

She sniffled a few times and a faint smile lit up her face. "I've got a plan." She took a few careful steps down the stairs, and Ryan looked down at her hands restrained by the tight ropes. In her left hand, the key to his handcuffs sparkled. She must have grabbed it from Moore when he picked her up.

The stale smell of bread consumed their lungs as they got deeper down into the main factory floor. It seemed like an eternity that Ryan first saw this vast abandoned space. They reached the bottom of the staircase. Mr Moore unbolted the front door, pushing each bar lock along to the wall like you would see in a shipping container. He sheepishly opened the front door and peered out onto the abandoned car park.

"All clear. Hurry up you two." Moore rushed out.

"Let me try to get you out," she whispered. Gabby slipped behind Ryan and tried his handcuffs with the key. It would be hard to unlock his handcuffs backwards. She missed the first time. Then, the clicks signalled that the rings were unlocked. They both gasped.

"Hurry up," Moore shouted from outside.

Ryan held the handcuffs behind his back, keeping up the appearance that he was still trapped. They shuffled out into the car park, Gabby's steps taking a second longer. He took a deep breath of the fresh air. The setting sun felt warm to his pale starved face. He squinted and the sun was like a welcome intruder. The surrounding hills of Thurlcaster in the far distance.

A helicopter appeared from over the hills. The distant sound of the propellers spinning causing a look of alarm on Mr Moore's face. He quickened his pace, still holding onto his trusty knife. They all hurriedly headed for the entrance gate. Ryan had to decide when the right time would be to make his move.

Mr Moore pulled out a rusted key and shoved it into the lock. The gates creaked open. His run-down 1999 Ford Fiesta was parked on the kerb outside. He stabbed the key into the driver side door. The doors unlocked with the locks popping up from their hideaways within the panels. He grabbed Gabby and she let out a roaring scream. Her mouth was quickly covered by his hand as he dragged her across the pavement and threw her into the passenger seat, before locking and slamming the door.

A screeching siren echoed all around them; Ryan's eyes searching for the source. A police car with blue lights appeared at the top of the road. It was driving in the middle of the road at such speed that it was hard to make out. Mr Moore grabbed Ryan and threw him in the back of the car, not noticing that Ryan didn't have the handcuffs on. Moore slid into the driver seat and the keys roared the engine into life.

The police car ground to an immediate halt next to them. DCI Binyon and PC Gables looked at them in horror. Moore pressed the accelerator and the car shot off down the road. Seizing his opportunity, Ryan leaned forward and grabbed the steering wheel.

"Get off, you'll kill us all."

The car swerved repeatedly across the road as they fought for control. Moore pushed Ryan and he fell back into his seat. He didn't know what else he could do. And then he saw it. He leaned back over and grabbed the hand brake that sat between Gabby and Moore and lifted it up. The car screeched as it ground to a stop.

Mr Moore looked around not knowing what was happening, and then saw Ryan's hand firmly on the brake.

"You little-"

Mr Moore flung the door open. DCI Binyon's car screeched to a stop again next to theirs. Mr Moore was now running down the road with his knife still in hand. Another four police cars flowed down the top of the road, all with their sirens on. The sound was deafening.

Ryan jumped out of the car following Moore. His knees rising up to his chest with each stride. It didn't take him long until he was a metre away from him. He propelled himself into the air, for a second feeling like he was flying, and landed on Moore's back. They collapsed to the hard pavement. Red wine blood leaked onto the path.

Nearby workers were now outside of their buildings watching the action, with dropped faces across the crowds. Police officers shot out of their cars and ran over to the scene. Ryan got up and saw that Moore's hand had clasped the blade of the knife and dug out a canal in his palm.

DCI Binyon forced handcuffs onto Mr Moore, grabbed the knife and lifted him up. A stream of blood continued to flow from his hand.

"We are placing you under arrest for the kidnapping and planned murder of Gabby Mcgee and Ryan Jones. You do not have to say anything. But it may harm your defence if you do not mention when questioned something which you later rely on in court."

They marched him over to the police car and hurled him into the back, the suspension of the car decompressing.

"Well done, Ryan," DCI Binyon said as she approached him. "I'm guessing it was your idea to let us know your location via Hito. The person on Hito also recorded the video footage on their mobile phone, so we have plenty of evidence against Bob Moore, alongside your testimonies of course."

Tears streamed down Gabby's face as the sirens remained feverishly high. Onlookers pointed towards the car as Gabby was removed from her restraints. Ryan watched as the police car carrying Mr Moore passed him. He locked eyes with him, and Ryan couldn't help but cast the biggest grin. He'd defeated him. Mr Moore looked at him before turning away to face the other side of the street. He knew he'd have to see him only once more, in court. The car drove into the distance, heading towards the setting sun.

Lorraine arrived soon after, both her and Gabby crying as they embraced each other. Each promising to do better in their role of daughter and mother. It was a long-awaited reunion. Lorraine smiled over at Ryan.

Waiting for his parents to arrive, he caught DCI Binyon standing with a tear in her eye.

"This makes it all worth it," she said, wiping her eyes clear.

He smiled up at her, her hair out of place from the action.

"Your first case solved. Did you really think I was the main suspect though?" he gazed at her as she tried to pull herself together.

She looked across the scene of emergency workers and cordons.

"I did," she said cheerlessly. "I knew you had more information than you gave us. And the pieces seemed to come together so well. The diary. You speaking to her on Hito. But all that probably says more about my inexperience than you as a suspect. You solved this case, not me."

He smiled at her.

A screeching appeared from the other side of the street, and he turned to see Mum lifting the cordon and running towards him. He couldn't help but whimper as he hugged her. He'd already imagined this moment so many times in his head. He hadn't prepared himself for the rush of emotions that flowed through his body.

His dad soon rushed to the scene too. All of them in a three-way family embrace which gave strength to Ryan's weakened body.

"We'll never be apart again," Mum said wiping tears from her face, "things will go back to being normal."

Things would never be "normal" again he thought. But that was a good thing. Normal before was being an outcast. Not anymore. He had orchestrated an investigation and pieced together clues to a mystery. He found Gabby. He bravely stood up to a criminal and brought him down. This was the new Ryan.

Epilogue

The controversial online game, Hito, has been sold to gaming company Ryder Global. The unknown creator of the game has reportedly made £450 million from the sale.

Marred with bad publicity, safety concerns over the game have been raised continuously. Three months ago, 14-year-old Gabby McGee from Thurlcaster was found after being missing for over two weeks. She was targeted by a teacher at her school, Robert Moore, who pretended to be a child in the game. He now awaits trial and is expected to face life imprisonment. He refuses to name his accomplices that helped operate a fraud hotline.

The police are investigating the game's safety policies, as well as others who are abusing the game. Depression has also risen in youngsters in the past year, with many speculating that this is because of the bullying that occurs in this anonymous virtual world.

Ryder Global have declined to comment on how they will approach safety concerns of the game but have said "we are delighted to welcome Hito into our eco-system of world-class games. We will continue to build upon the game to make it evermore appealing to users."

Ryan and Cali sat in the corner of the canteen. Cali's hair catching the morning sun. He lifted his head from the newspaper, looking at the sea of the students all dressed in their pristine uniforms. Black blazers and crisp new white shirts. Ryan smiled.

"Look at that grin!" Cali said taking a bite from an apple, "I think this is the happiest you've ever been to return to school."

"I guess it is."

"I'm happy too. But I can't stop thinking about my aunt's wedding this weekend. My mum told all of them about Max, and now the only thing I'm hearing is how excited they are to meet him. Especially the ones flying over from Ghana."

"Wait – you can't have this both ways! Think back to a few months ago when you were so scared of any-one knowing."

Cali's eyes glinted and a small smile grew on his face.

"There you are!" a voice shouted. He looked up and Max was heading towards their table. His tall physique standing out against the tiny figures. He gripped a newspaper in his hand. He reached their table and plonked himself down.

"Hey, handsome," he said, looking at Cali. Ryan loved seeing how open his friends could be.

"Did you see Hito has been sold?" He faced Ryan, putting the newspaper on the table.

Ryan nodded and placed his copy on the table. "I was just reading it. Remember - don't mention it to Gabby."

Max nodded knowingly.

"So...Liam's party on Saturday. You in, mate?"

"Annabel's, right?" Ryan said, fidgeting with his hands.

Max nodded.

"I guess I am," Ryan said. He remembered how he was the outcast a few months ago, and now he was invited to all the cool parties.

"Hide that!" Max grabbed the newspapers on the table and stuffed them under his seat. Ryan couldn't comprehend fast enough why he was doing that.

"Morning," a voice said. Ryan looked up and saw Gabby standing beside him. He got up from his chair and gently kissed her on the lips.

"Get a room!" Cali said as he and Max laughed. Ryan and Gabby smirked as they sat down.

They'd both been inseparable since the incident. When they weren't with each other, they spent their time chatting on MSN or speaking on the phone until late, with one of them often falling asleep mid-sentence.

"What were you talking about before I came?" Gabby asked, her eyes looking around the group.

Ryan was about to reply when the canteen descended into hush. All of the chatter from the tables silenced. The sizzling of the fryer was the only noise to be heard. Footsteps appeared from the other side of the room. His view was blocked. He moved from left to right but still had no luck. The footsteps were approaching the canteen counter.

"Black coffee, please, Margaret." Mr Dhanial's voice broke the room's silence—the coffee machine shot to life. The students stared at Mr Dhanial; the pack followed each movement he made. This was the jungle, and he was prey. Ryan stood up so he could get a clear view. Margaret handed him the coffee without saying a word, and he marched back through the canteen with his head down. A few boos bounced around the room as he walked through the crowds.

"You're a disgrace!" a voice shouted. Mr Dhanial picked up pace and scuttled out of the canteen doors. The room burst back into life, and the chatter brought the room back to an average level. The hunt was finished. Their target gone.

The kids blamed Mr Dhanial for hiring Moore in the first place. All the students believe he must have known what he was up to or should have at least had a better vetting process in place for staff.

"Rumour has it, he has already resigned and is heading to a different school. He definitely knew about Moore," Max said.

Gabby tremored. Her hands shaking.

"Sorry," Max said with an apologetic smile.

Some people began filtering out as lesson time neared. The sea of blue plastic chairs becoming more prominent, and the sand-coloured tables now visible again. The canteen didn't look as much like a sad holiday resort as it used to.

Tina walked past the group with her tray.

"Oh my god, he is such a loser," she said, speaking to Jasmine, who was walking beside her, "And what kind of a name is Paul? It's a middle-aged man's name." She and Jasmine laughed.

Gabby gave a civil smile to Tina. A smile suitable for an acquaintance who was once something more.

The bell started ringing. The ticker manically hit the base, angrily telling the whole room it was time for the next class and that break was over. After six weeks of school holidays, lazing around each day, and watching cartoons, it would take a day or two for the usual rush of the hallways to return.

All four of them stood up and headed to English Literature class. Doing this lesson in the same classroom they were in before would be weird. This time, thankfully, with a new teacher.

Butterflies flitted through the late summer air, filled with the smell of freshly cut grass for the last time before autumn set in. Brand new leather shoes squeaked as pupils shuffled into classrooms to receive new exercise books. They resolved to write their very neatest...at least to start with.

Ryan's life was changed forever by Hito. Some of it was awful. He wishes he could forget being tied up and having that fear of being murdered at only fourteen years old. In some ways, he was thankful for what he had gone through and saw it as the making of him being who he is now.

He wondered how Hito would be now that Ryder had bought it. One thing was for certain – their story wouldn't be the last of the destruction. Not until everyone operating the pay scheme was caught. And even then, the game could easily be exploited in other ways.

###

About The Author

Cameron Lawrence is a writer from the North East of England. He currently resides in Hastings by the sea with his partner and enjoys taking long walks along the pebble beach when he is not writing.

www.ingramcontent.com/pod-product-compliance
Lightning Source LLC
Chambersburg PA
CBHW060711190726

48289CB00002B/637